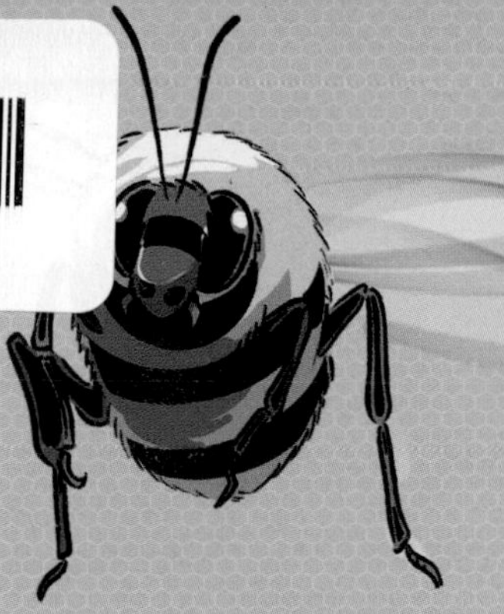

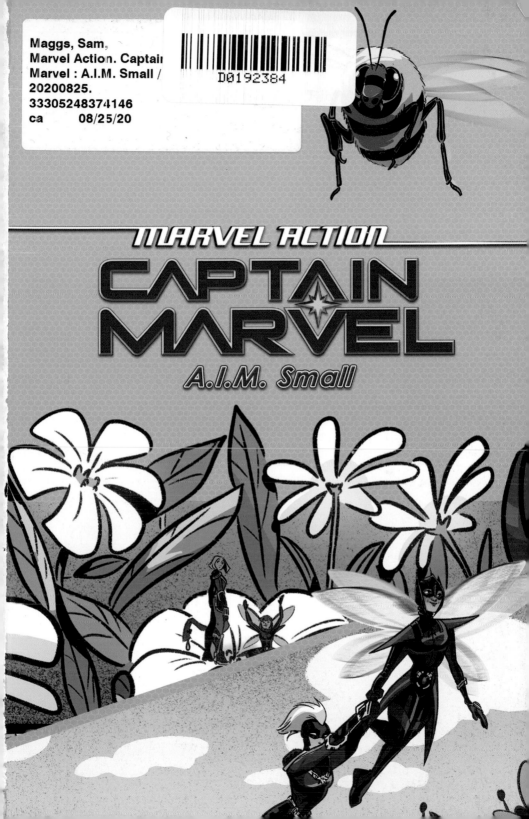

MARVEL ACTION
CAPTAIN MARVEL
A.I.M. Small

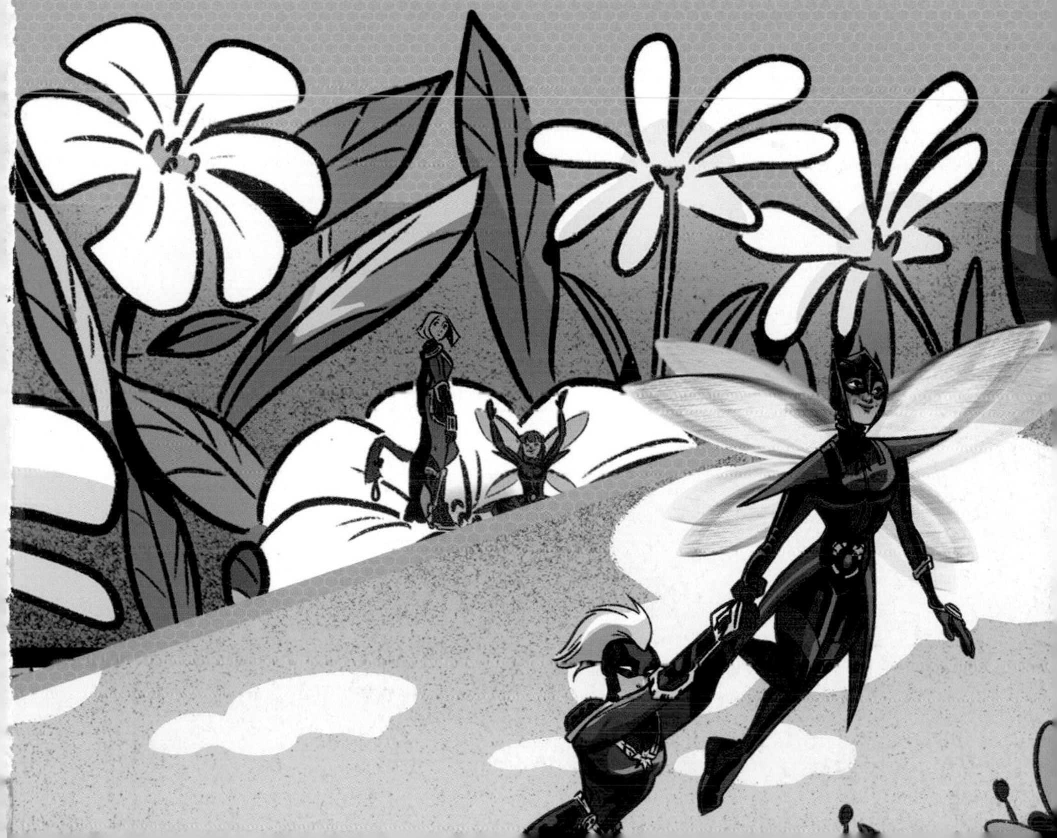

MARVEL — MARVEL ACTION
CAPTAIN MARVEL

Marvel Publishing:

Jeff Youngquist: VP Production & Special Projects
Lauren Bisom: Editor, Juvenile Publishing
Caitlin O'Connell: Assistant Editor, Special Projects
Sven Larsen: VP, Licensed Publishing
David Gabriel: SVP Print, Sales & Marketing
Joe Quesada: Chief Creative Officer
C.B. Cebulski: Editor In Chief

IDW Publishing:

Chris Ryall, President and Publisher/CCO
Cara Morrison, Chief Financial Officer
Matt Ruzicka, Chief Accounting Officer
John Barber, Editor-In-Chief
Justin Eisinger, Editorial Director, Graphic Novels & Collections
Jerry Bennington, VP of New Product Development
Lorelei Bunjes, VP of Digital Services
Jud Meyers, Sales Director
Anna Morrow, Marketing Director
Tara McCrillis, Director of Design & Production
Mike Ford, Director of Operations
Shauna Monteforte, Manufacturing Operations Director
Rebekah Cahalin, General Manager
Ted Adams and **Robbie Robbins,** Founders of IDW

Cover Artist
SWEENEY BOO

Series Editors
MEGAN BROWN
and **BOBBY CURNOW**

Collection Editors
ALONZO SIMON
and **ZAC BOONE**

Collection Designer
CHRISTA MIESNER

ISBN: 978-1-68405-684-2   23 22 21 20   1 2 3 4

Special thanks: **Sana Amanat** and **Sarah Brunstad**.

MARVEL ACTION: CAPTAIN MARVEL: A.I.M. SMALL (BOOK TWO). AUGUST 2020.
FIRST PRINTING. © 2020 MARVEL. The IDW logo is registered in the U.S. Patent and
Trademark Office. IDW Publishing, a division of Idea and Design Works, LLC. Editorial offices:
2765 Truxtun Road, San Diego, CA 92106. Any similarities to persons living or dead are purely
coincidental. With the exception of artwork used for review purposes, none of the contents
of this publication may be reprinted without the permission of Idea and Design Works, LLC.

Printed in Korea.

IDW Publishing does not read or accept unsolicited submissions
of ideas, stories, or artwork.

Originally published as MARVEL ACTION: CAPTAIN MARVEL issues #4–6.

WRITTEN BY
SAM MAGGS

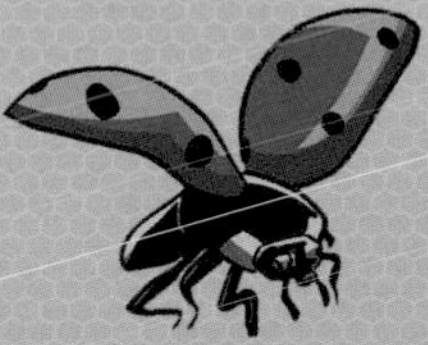

ART BY
SWEENEY BOO

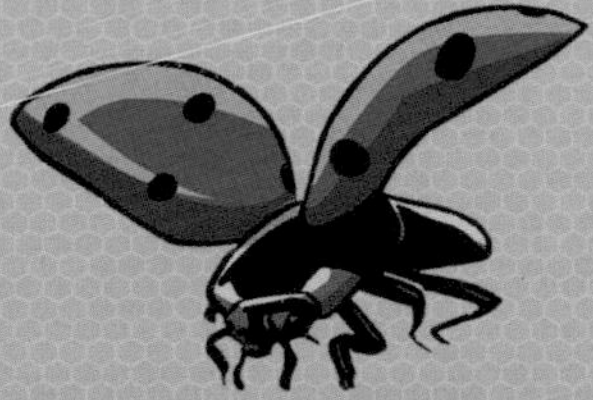

COLORS BY
BRITTANY PEER

LETTERS BY CHRISTA MIESNER

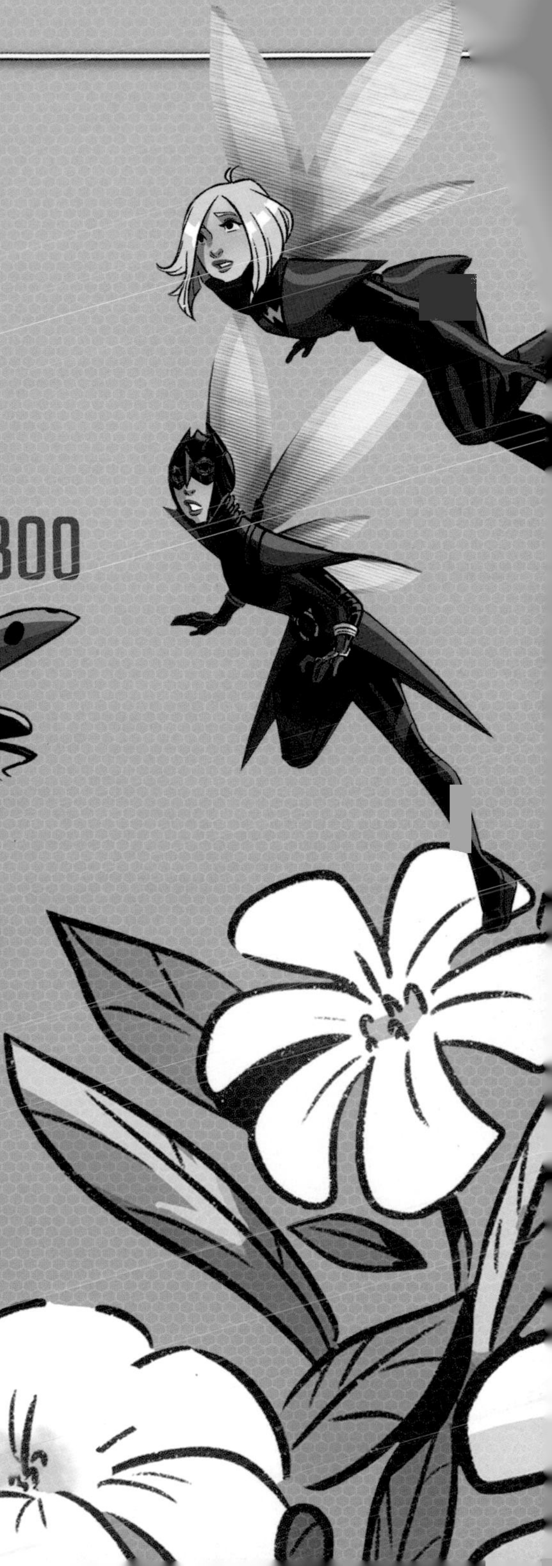

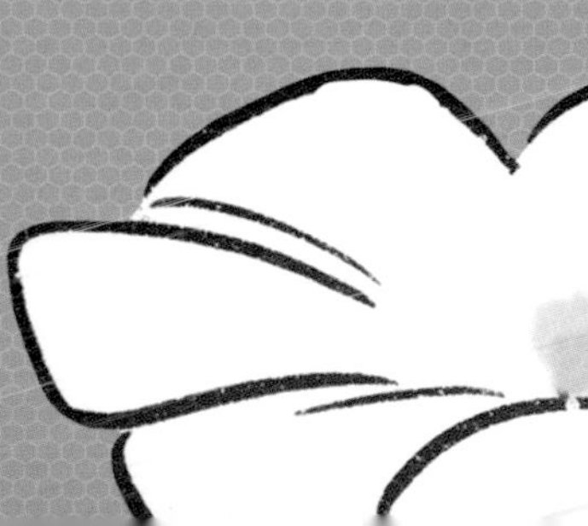

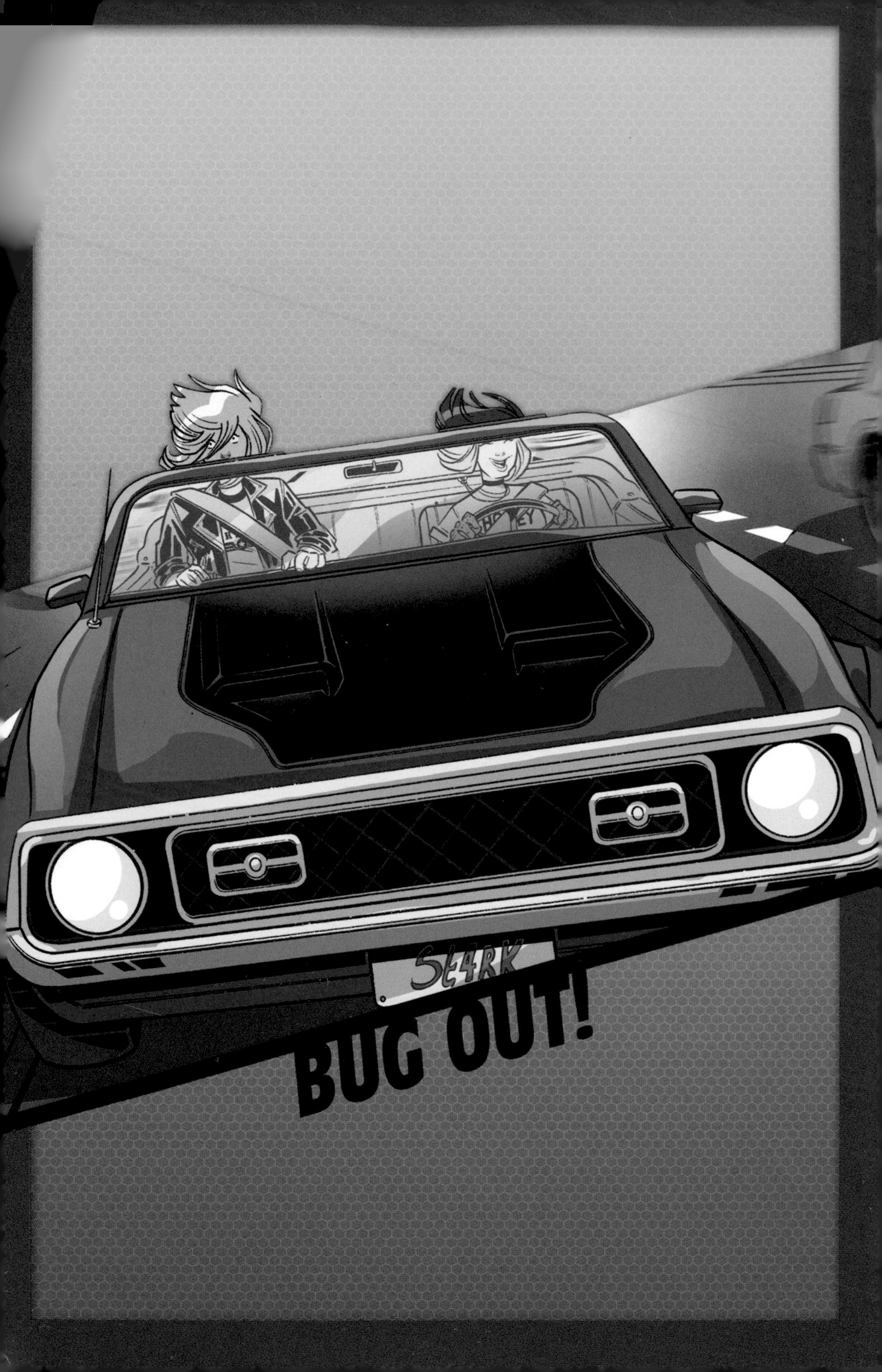
SE4RK
BUG OUT!

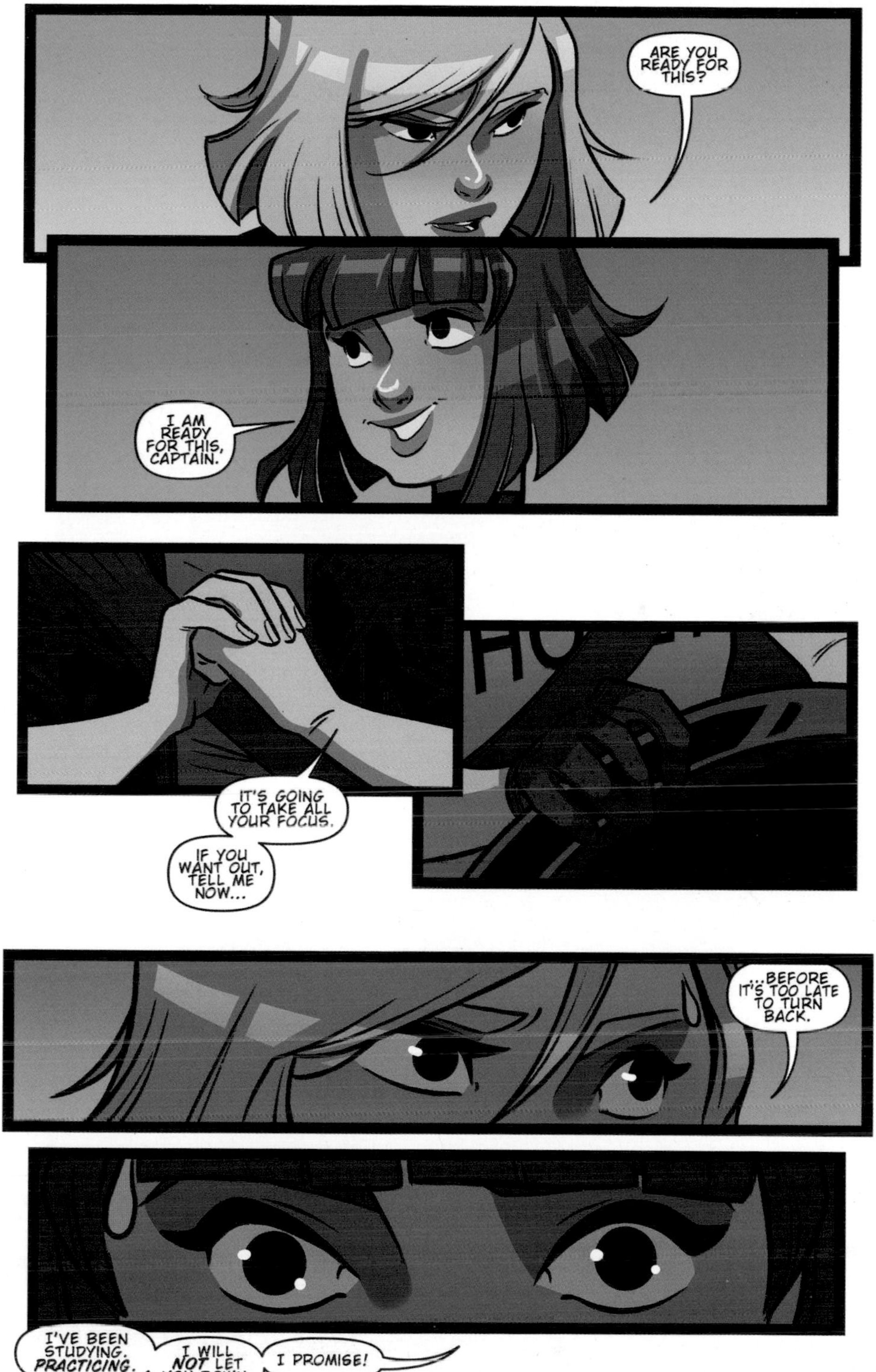
ARE YOU READY FOR THIS?
I AM READY FOR THIS, CAPTAIN.
IT'S GOING TO TAKE ALL YOUR FOCUS.
IF YOU WANT OUT, TELL ME NOW...
...BEFORE IT'S TOO LATE TO TURN BACK.
I'VE BEEN STUDYING. PRACTICING.
I WILL NOT LET YOU DOWN.
I PROMISE!

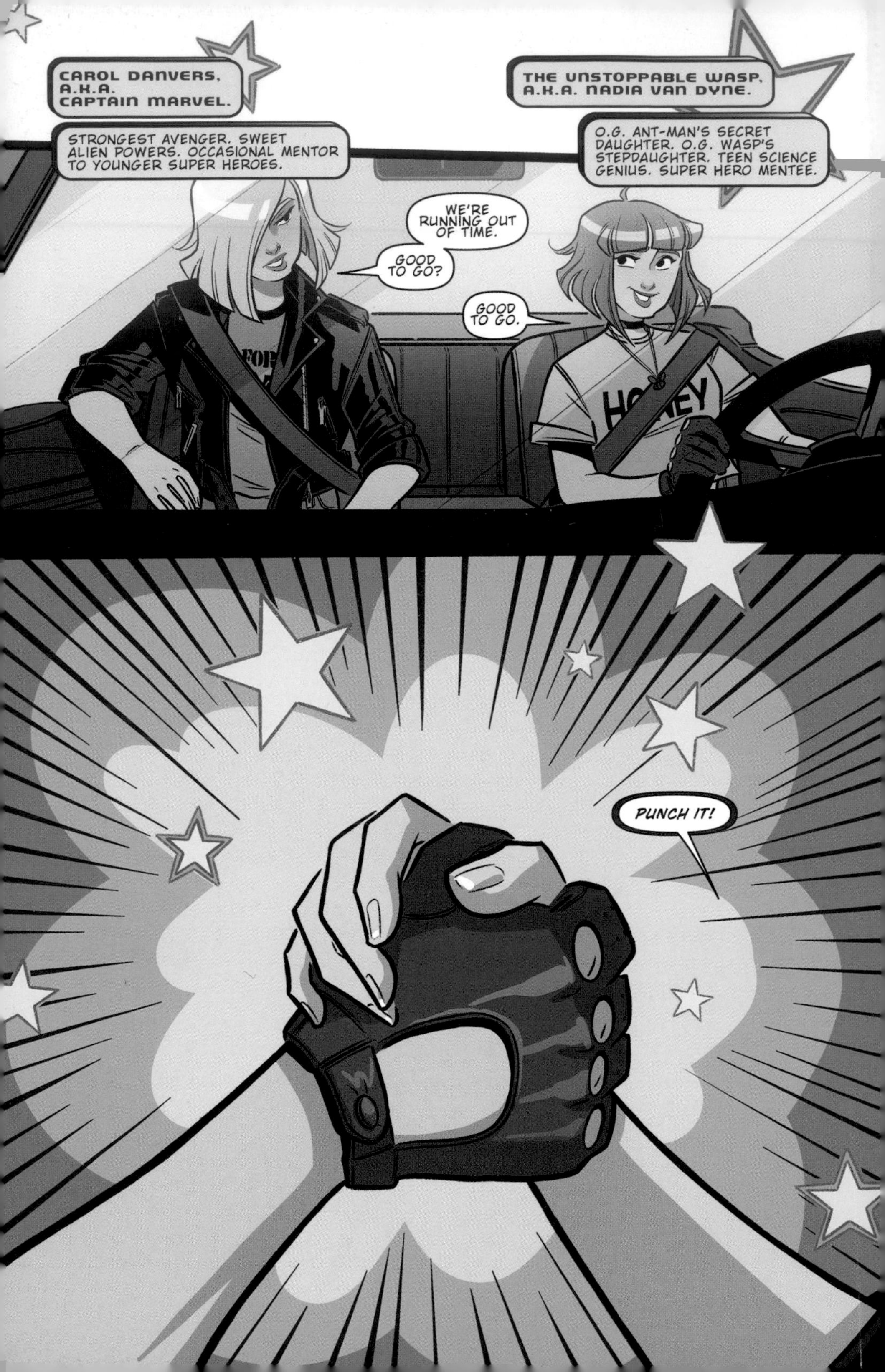
CAROL DANVERS, A.K.A. CAPTAIN MARVEL.
STRONGEST AVENGER. SWEET ALIEN POWERS. OCCASIONAL MENTOR TO YOUNGER SUPER HEROES.
THE UNSTOPPABLE WASP, A.K.A. NADIA VAN DYNE.
O.G. ANT-MAN'S SECRET DAUGHTER. O.G. WASP'S STEPDAUGHTER. TEEN SCIENCE GENIUS. SUPER HERO MENTEE.
WE'RE RUNNING OUT OF TIME.
GOOD TO GO?
GOOD TO GO.
PUNCH IT!

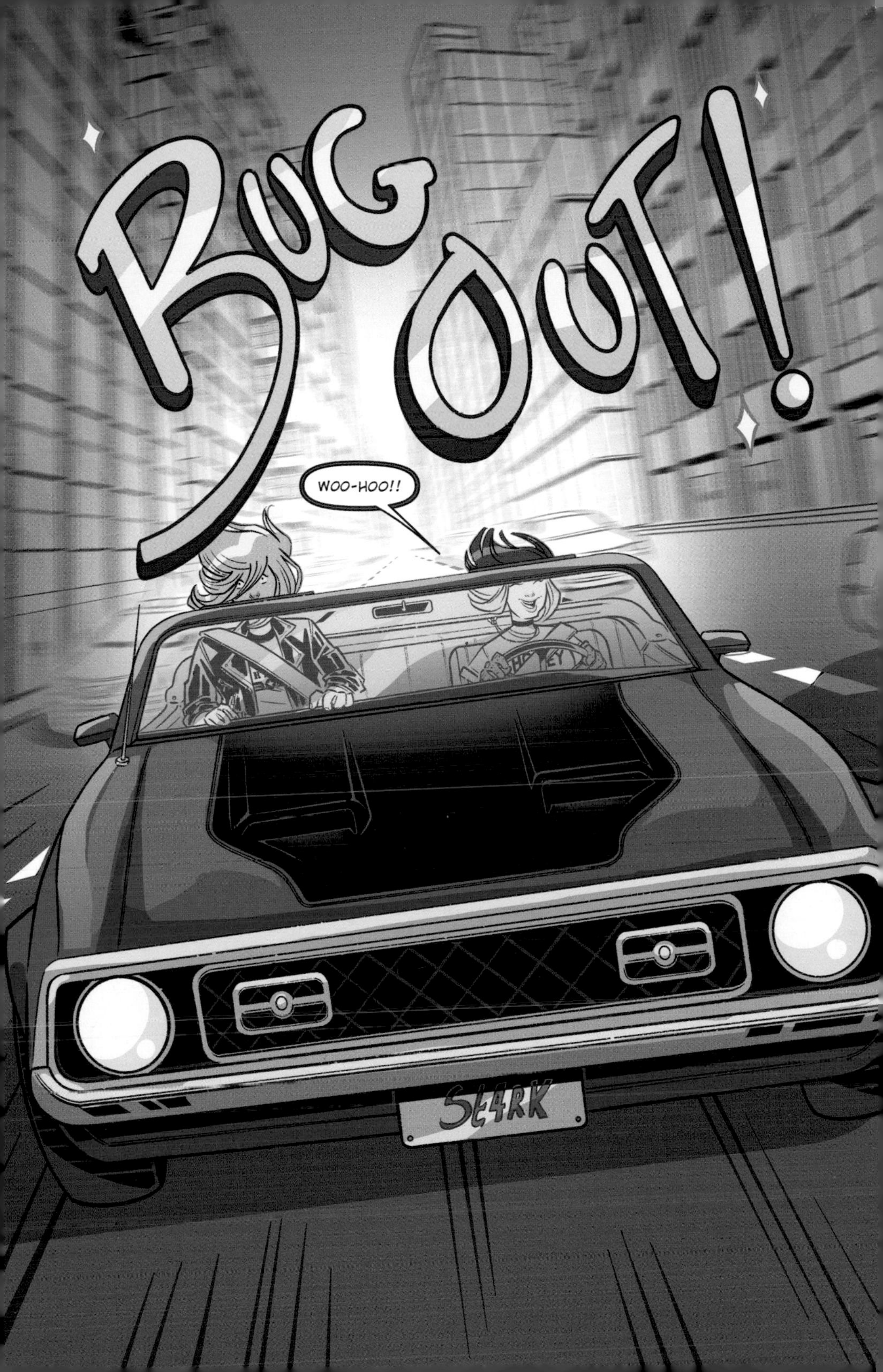
BUG OUT!
WOO-HOO!!
SE4RK

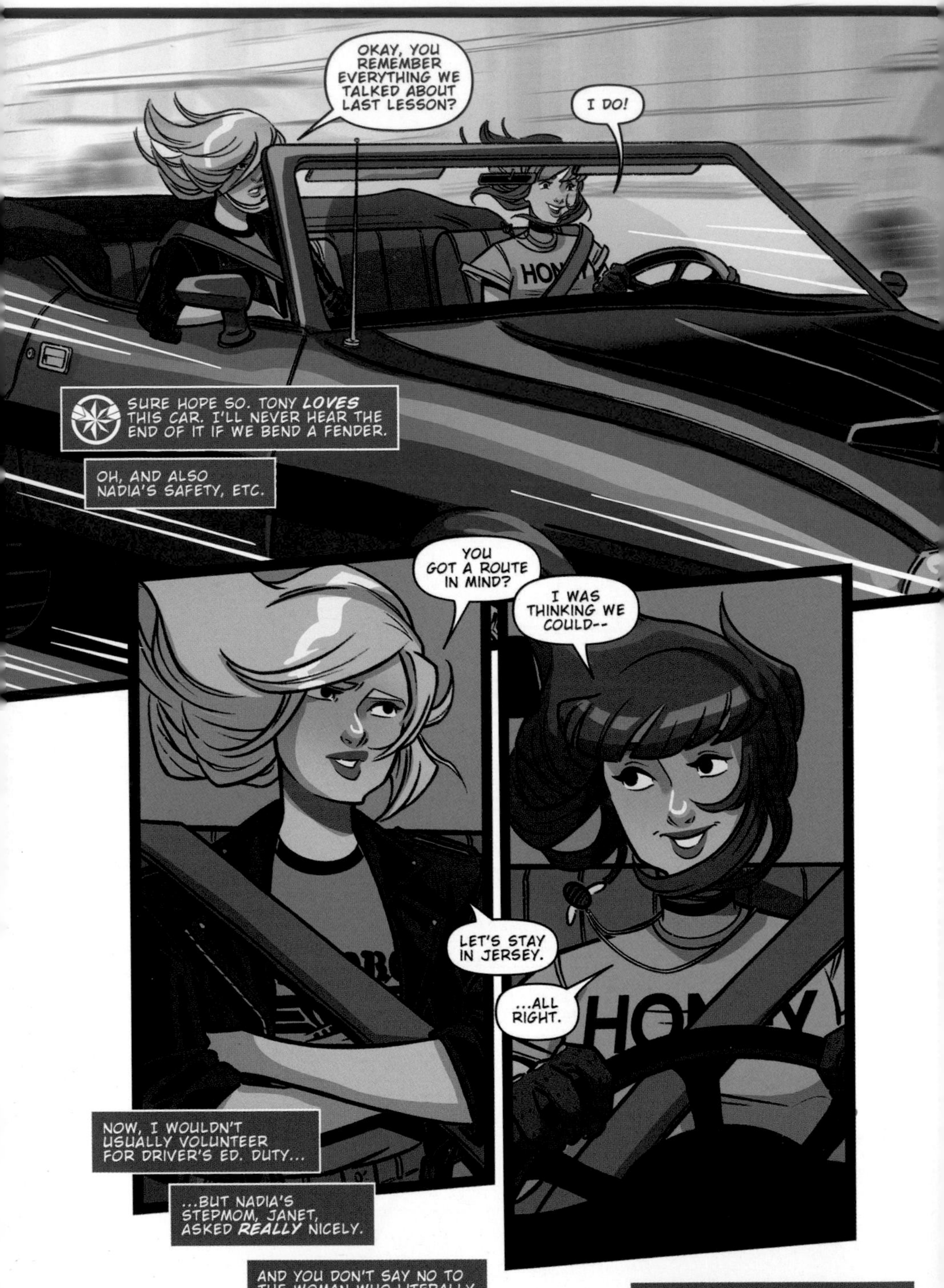

OKAY, YOU REMEMBER EVERYTHING WE TALKED ABOUT LAST LESSON?
I DO!
SURE HOPE SO. TONY LOVES THIS CAR. I'LL NEVER HEAR THE END OF IT IF WE BEND A FENDER.
OH, AND ALSO NADIA'S SAFETY, ETC.
YOU GOT A ROUTE IN MIND?
I WAS THINKING WE COULD--
LET'S STAY IN JERSEY.
...ALL RIGHT.
NOW, I WOULDN'T USUALLY VOLUNTEER FOR DRIVER'S ED. DUTY...
...BUT NADIA'S STEPMOM, JANET, ASKED REALLY NICELY.
AND YOU DON'T SAY NO TO THE WOMAN WHO LITERALLY NAMED THE AVENGERS.
(ESPECIALLY NOT AFTER YOU LOSE A PARTICULARLY DEVASTATING POKER GAME TO HER.)

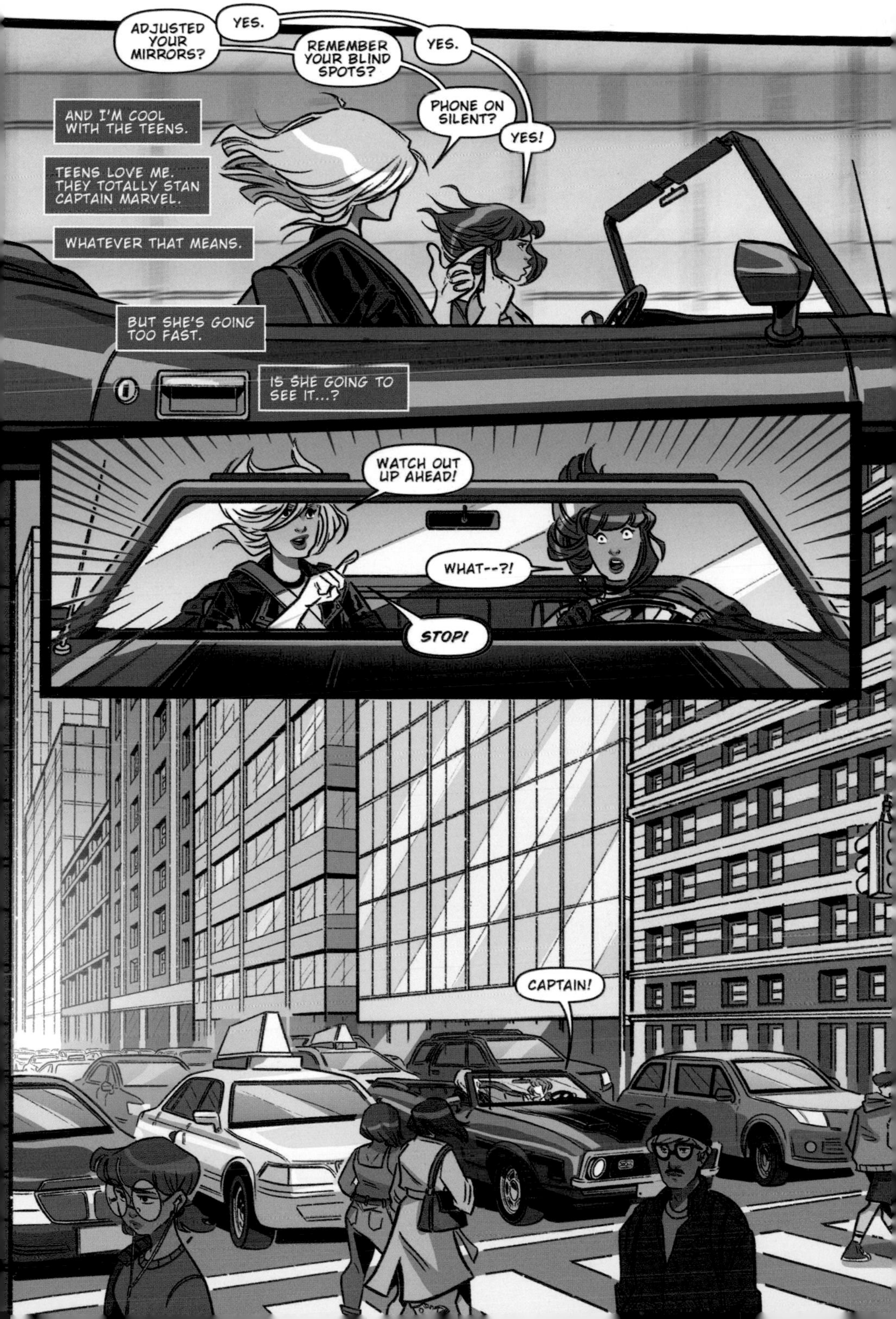
ADJUSTED YOUR MIRRORS?
YES.
REMEMBER YOUR BLIND SPOTS?
YES.
PHONE ON SILENT?
YES!
AND I'M COOL WITH THE TEENS.
TEENS LOVE ME. THEY TOTALLY STAN CAPTAIN MARVEL.
WHATEVER THAT MEANS.
BUT SHE'S GOING TOO FAST.
IS SHE GOING TO SEE IT...?
WATCH OUT UP AHEAD!
WHAT--?!
STOP!
CAPTAIN!

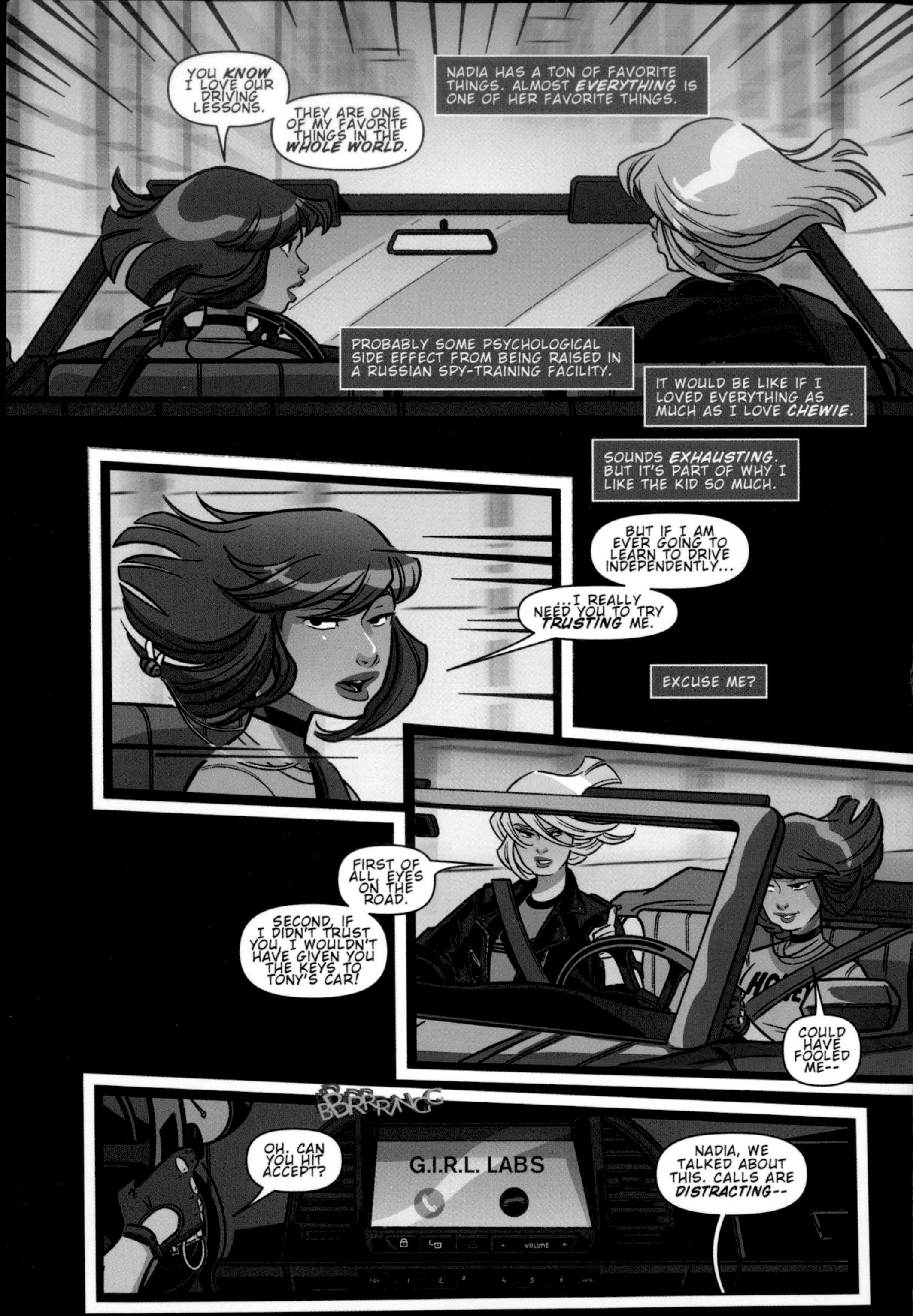

YOU KNOW I LOVE OUR DRIVING LESSONS.
THEY ARE ONE OF MY FAVORITE THINGS IN THE WHOLE WORLD.
NADIA HAS A TON OF FAVORITE THINGS. ALMOST EVERYTHING IS ONE OF HER FAVORITE THINGS.
PROBABLY SOME PSYCHOLOGICAL SIDE EFFECT FROM BEING RAISED IN A RUSSIAN SPY-TRAINING FACILITY.
IT WOULD BE LIKE IF I LOVED EVERYTHING AS MUCH AS I LOVE CHEWIE.
SOUNDS EXHAUSTING. BUT IT'S PART OF WHY I LIKE THE KID SO MUCH.
BUT IF I AM EVER GOING TO LEARN TO DRIVE INDEPENDENTLY...
...I REALLY NEED YOU TO TRY TRUSTING ME.
EXCUSE ME?
FIRST OF ALL, EYES ON THE ROAD.
SECOND, IF I DIDN'T TRUST YOU, I WOULDN'T HAVE GIVEN YOU THE KEYS TO TONY'S CAR!
COULD HAVE FOOLED ME--
BBRRRRNG
OH. CAN YOU HIT ACCEPT?
G.I.R.L. LABS
VOLUME
NADIA, WE TALKED ABOUT THIS. CALLS ARE DISTRACTING--

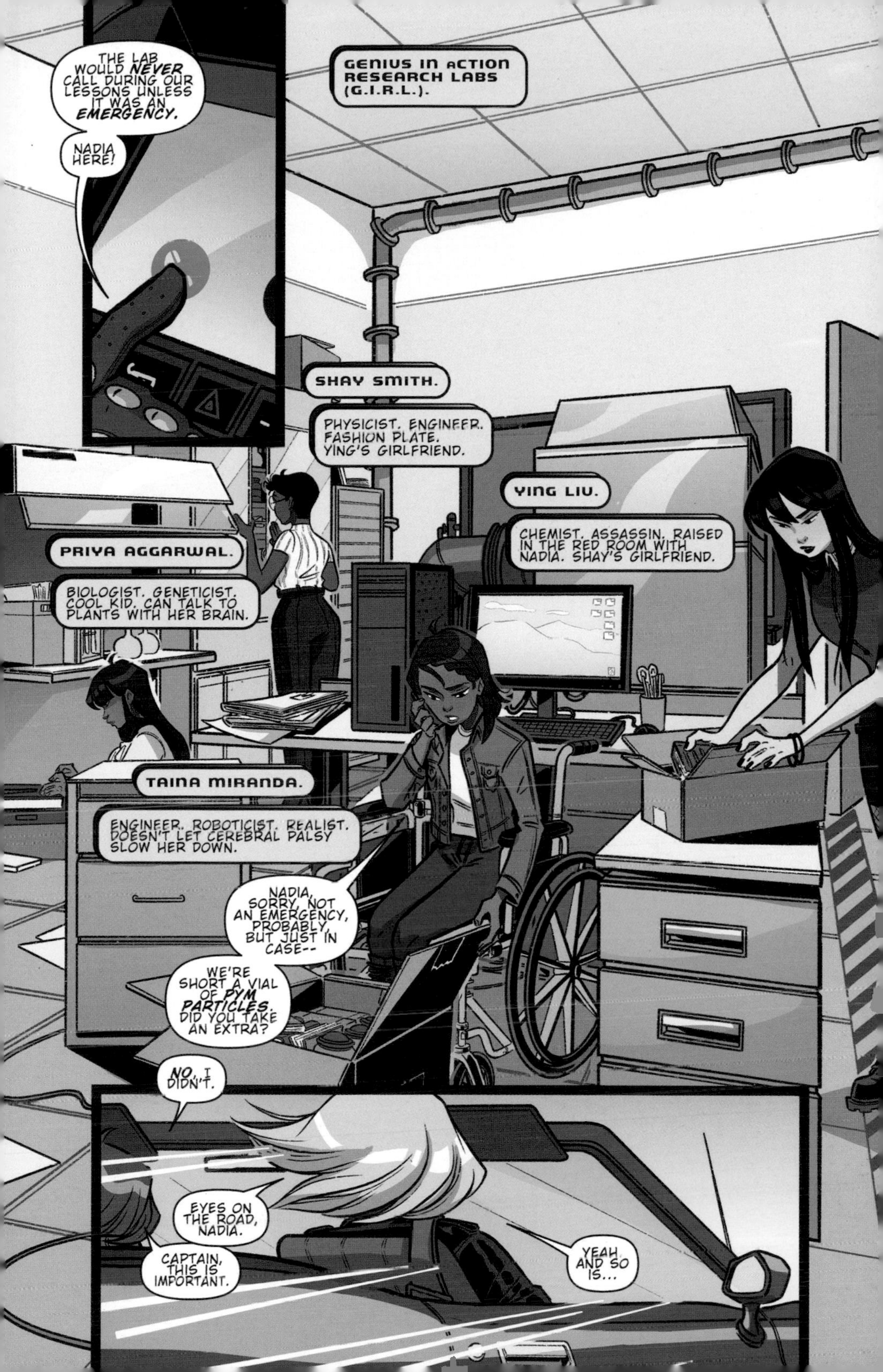
THE LAB WOULD *NEVER* CALL DURING OUR LESSONS UNLESS IT WAS AN *EMERGENCY.*
NADIA HERE!
GENIUS IN ACTION RESEARCH LABS (G.I.R.L.).
SHAY SMITH.
PHYSICIST. ENGINEER. FASHION PLATE. YING'S GIRLFRIEND.
YING LIU.
CHEMIST. ASSASSIN. RAISED IN THE RED ROOM WITH NADIA. SHAY'S GIRLFRIEND.
PRIYA AGGARWAL.
BIOLOGIST. GENETICIST. COOL KID. CAN TALK TO PLANTS WITH HER BRAIN.
TAINA MIRANDA.
ENGINEER. ROBOTICIST. REALIST. DOESN'T LET CEREBRAL PALSY SLOW HER DOWN.
NADIA, SORRY, NOT AN EMERGENCY, PROBABLY, BUT JUST IN CASE--
WE'RE SHORT A VIAL OF *PYM PARTICLES.* DID YOU TAKE AN EXTRA?
NO, I DIDN'T.
EYES ON THE ROAD, NADIA.
CAPTAIN, THIS IS IMPORTANT.
YEAH, AND SO IS...

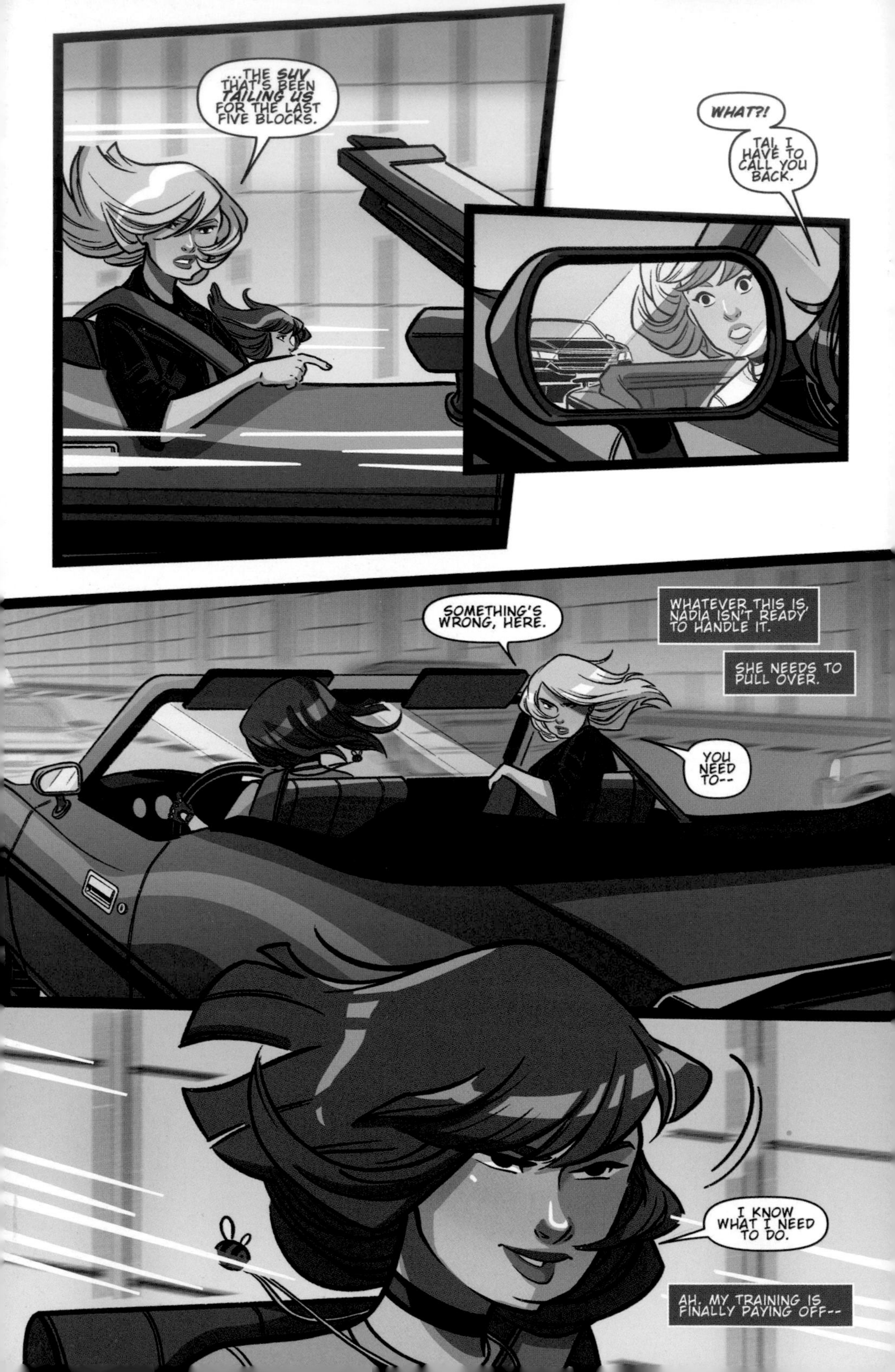
...THE SUV THAT'S BEEN TAILING US FOR THE LAST FIVE BLOCKS.
WHAT?!
TAI, I HAVE TO CALL YOU BACK.
SOMETHING'S WRONG, HERE.
WHATEVER THIS IS, NADIA ISN'T READY TO HANDLE IT.
SHE NEEDS TO PULL OVER.
YOU NEED TO--
I KNOW WHAT I NEED TO DO.
AH. MY TRAINING IS FINALLY PAYING OFF--

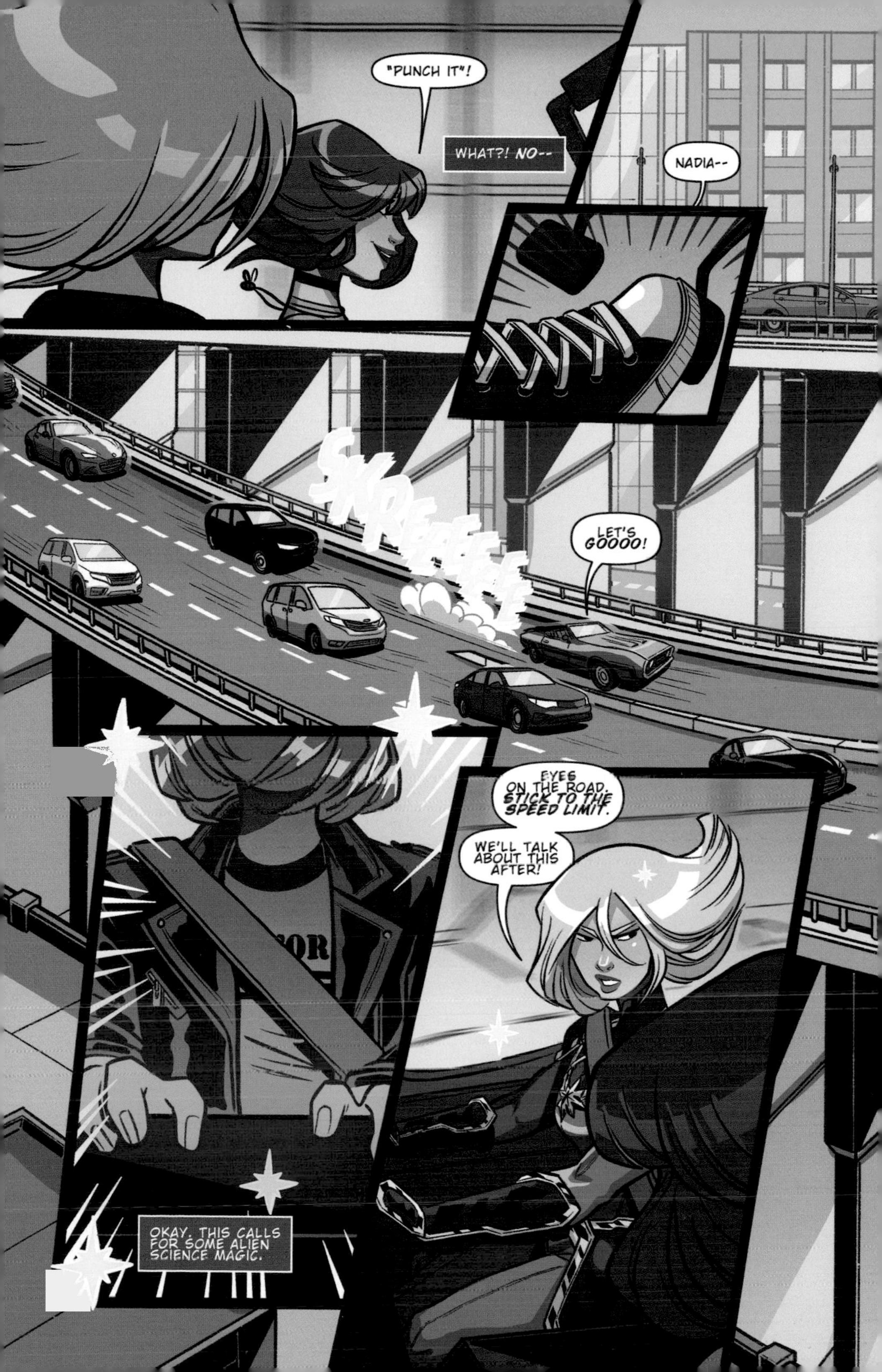
"PUNCH IT"!
WHAT?! NO--
NADIA--
SKREEEEEE
LET'S GOOOO!
EYES ON THE ROAD. STICK TO THE SPEED LIMIT.
WE'LL TALK ABOUT THIS AFTER!
OKAY. THIS CALLS FOR SOME ALIEN SCIENCE MAGIC.

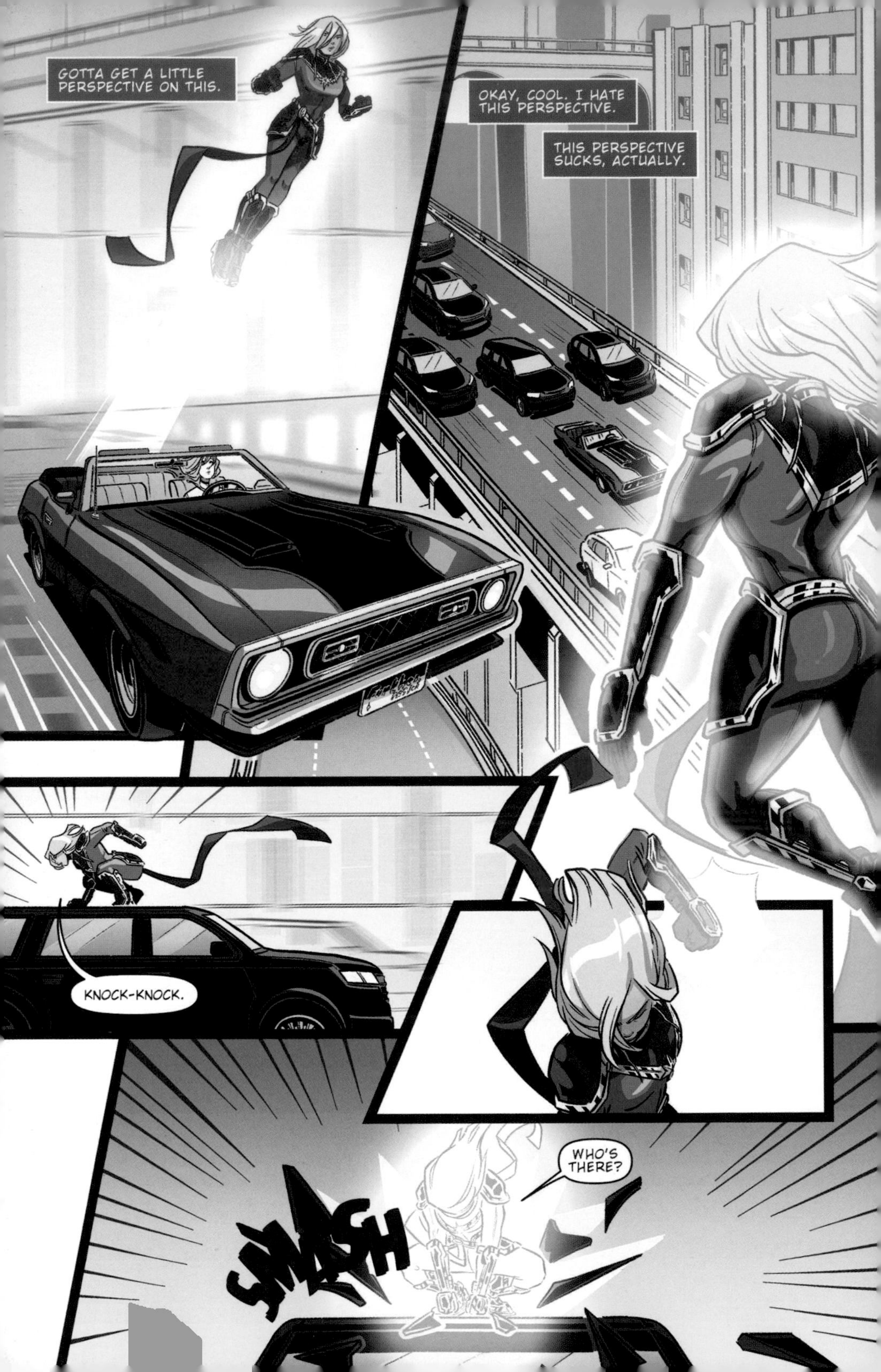
GOTTA GET A LITTLE PERSPECTIVE ON THIS.
OKAY, COOL. I HATE THIS PERSPECTIVE.
THIS PERSPECTIVE SUCKS, ACTUALLY.
KNOCK-KNOCK.
WHO'S THERE?
SMASH

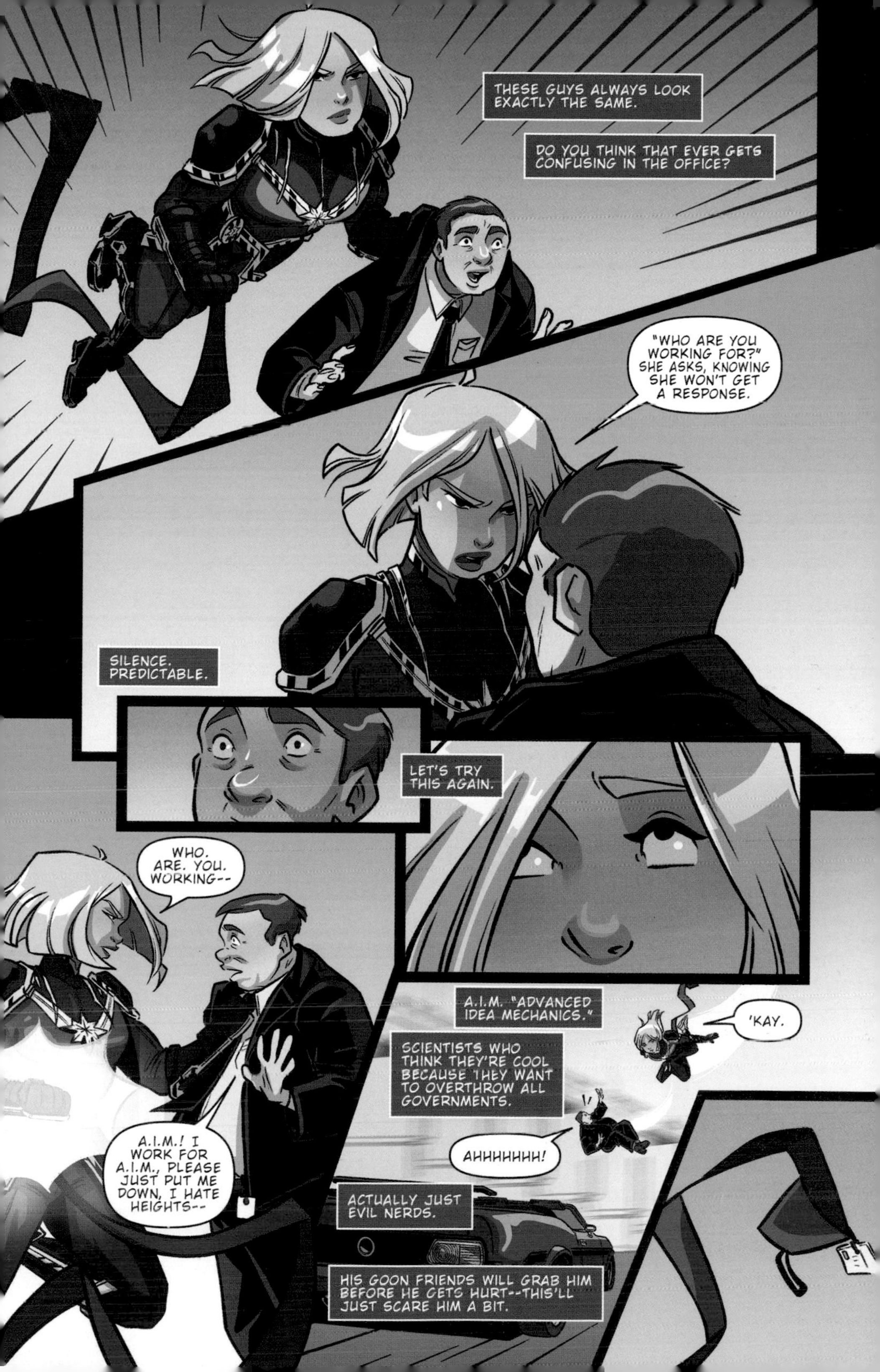
THESE GUYS ALWAYS LOOK EXACTLY THE SAME.
DO YOU THINK THAT EVER GETS CONFUSING IN THE OFFICE?
"WHO ARE YOU WORKING FOR?" SHE ASKS, KNOWING SHE WON'T GET A RESPONSE.
SILENCE. PREDICTABLE.
LET'S TRY THIS AGAIN.
WHO. ARE. YOU. WORKING--
A.I.M.! I WORK FOR A.I.M., PLEASE JUST PUT ME DOWN, I HATE HEIGHTS--
A.I.M. "ADVANCED IDEA MECHANICS."
SCIENTISTS WHO THINK THEY'RE COOL BECAUSE THEY WANT TO OVERTHROW ALL GOVERNMENTS.
'KAY.
AHHHHHHH!
ACTUALLY JUST EVIL NERDS.
HIS GOON FRIENDS WILL GRAB HIM BEFORE HE GETS HURT--THIS'LL JUST SCARE HIM A BIT.

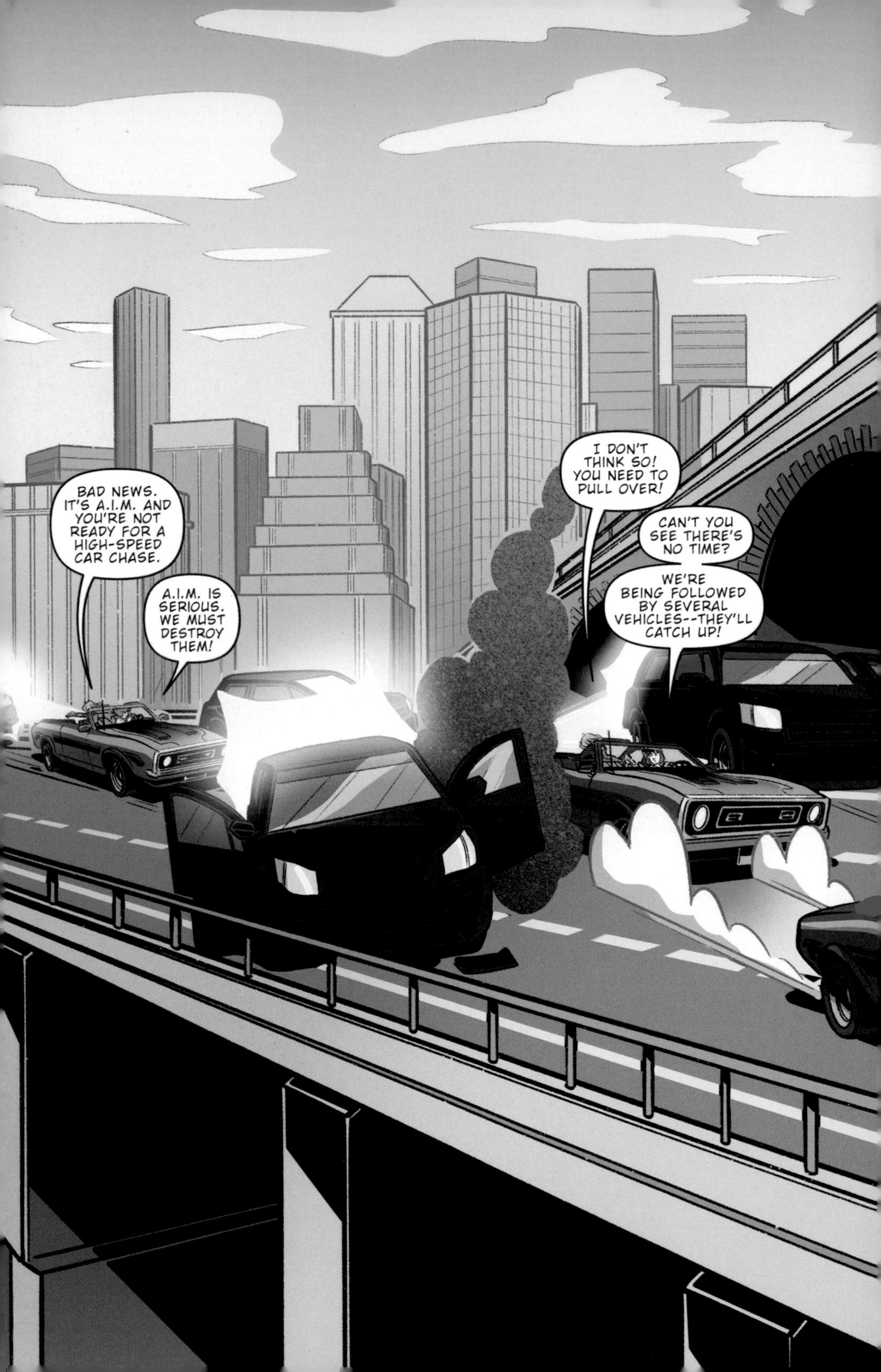
BAD NEWS. IT'S A.I.M. AND YOU'RE NOT READY FOR A HIGH-SPEED CAR CHASE.
A.I.M. IS SERIOUS. WE MUST DESTROY THEM!
I DON'T THINK SO! YOU NEED TO PULL OVER!
CAN'T YOU SEE THERE'S NO TIME?
WE'RE BEING FOLLOWED BY SEVERAL VEHICLES--THEY'LL CATCH UP!

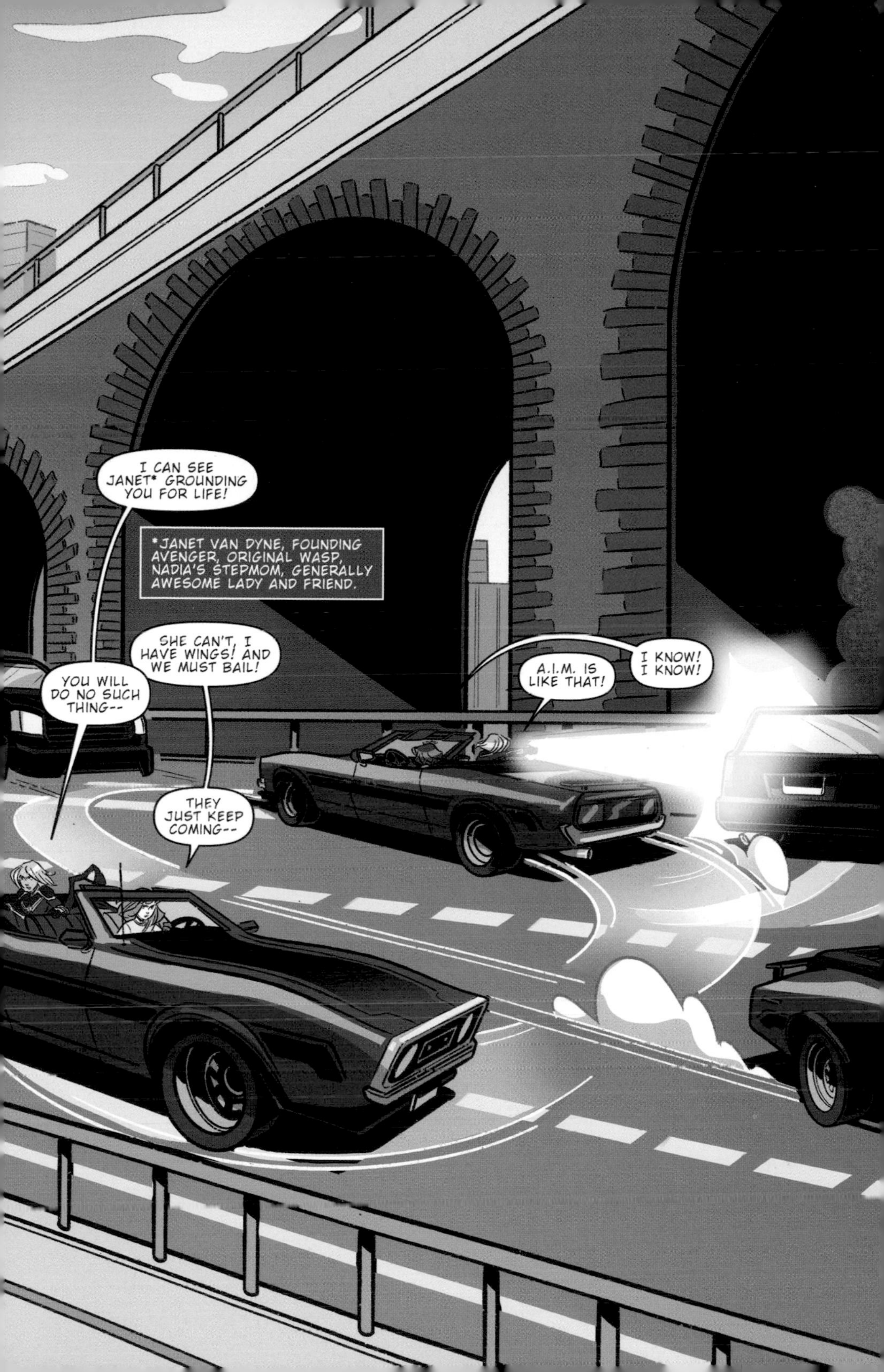
I CAN SEE JANET* GROUNDING YOU FOR LIFE!
*JANET VAN DYNE, FOUNDING AVENGER, ORIGINAL WASP, NADIA'S STEPMOM, GENERALLY AWESOME LADY AND FRIEND.
YOU WILL DO NO SUCH THING--
SHE CAN'T, I HAVE WINGS! AND WE MUST BAIL!
THEY JUST KEEP COMING--
A.I.M. IS LIKE THAT!
I KNOW! I KNOW!

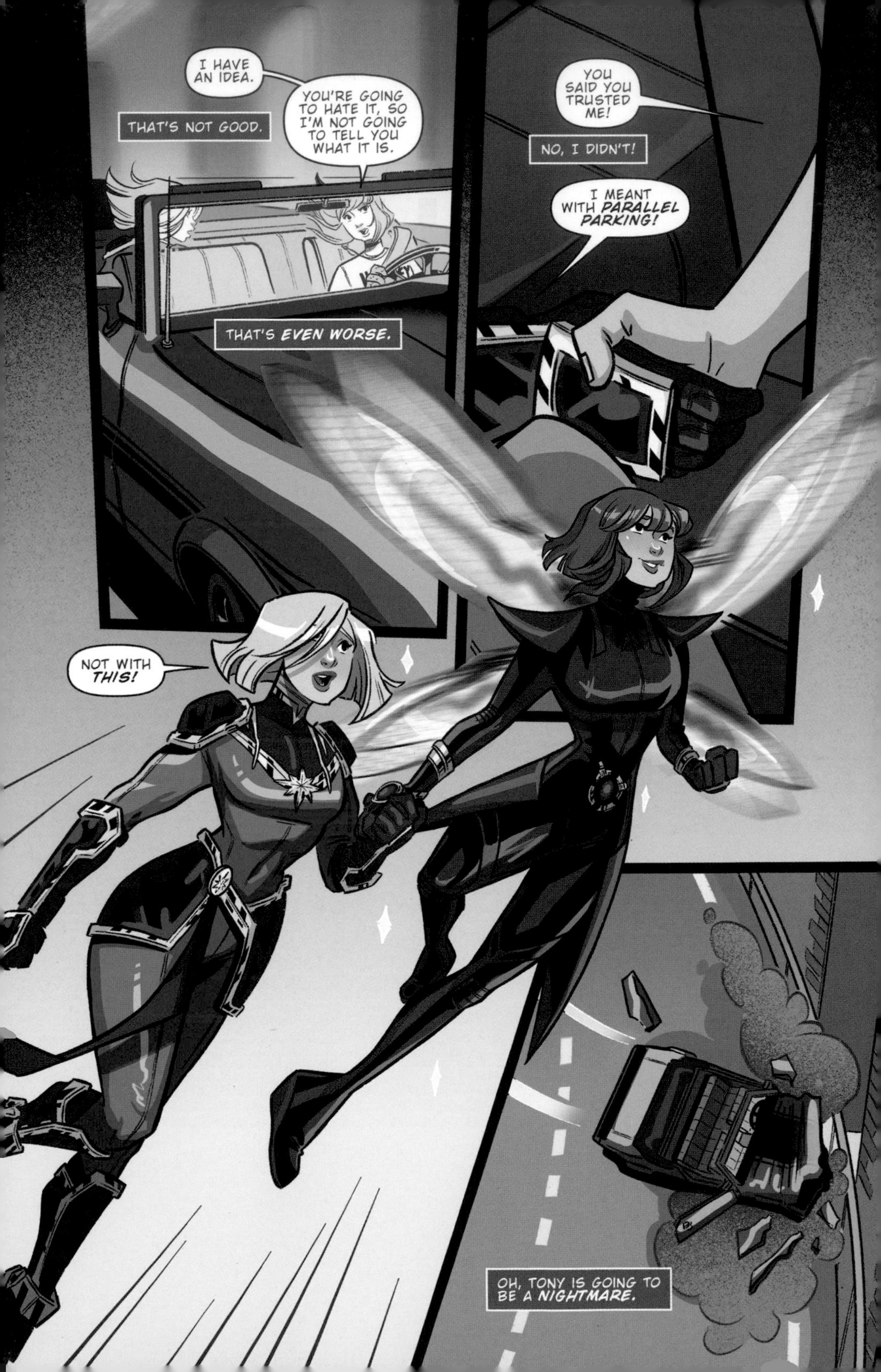

I HAVE AN IDEA.
THAT'S NOT GOOD.
YOU'RE GOING TO HATE IT, SO I'M NOT GOING TO TELL YOU WHAT IT IS.
THAT'S EVEN WORSE.
YOU SAID YOU TRUSTED ME!
NO, I DIDN'T!
I MEANT WITH PARALLEL PARKING!
NOT WITH THIS!
OH, TONY IS GOING TO BE A NIGHTMARE.

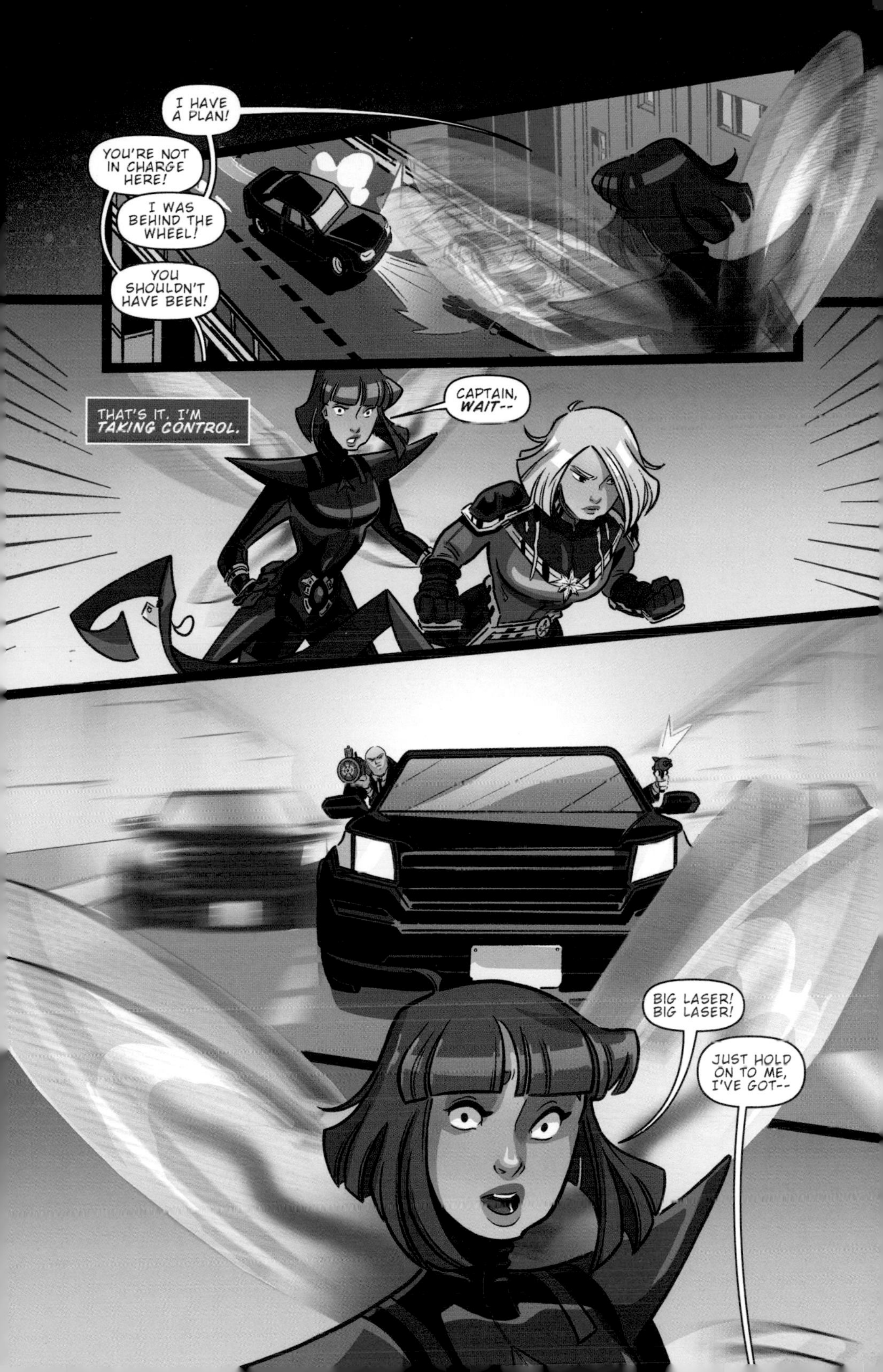
I HAVE A PLAN!
YOU'RE NOT IN CHARGE HERE!
I WAS BEHIND THE WHEEL!
YOU SHOULDN'T HAVE BEEN!
THAT'S IT. I'M TAKING CONTROL.
CAPTAIN, WAIT--
BIG LASER! BIG LASER!
JUST HOLD ON TO ME, I'VE GOT--

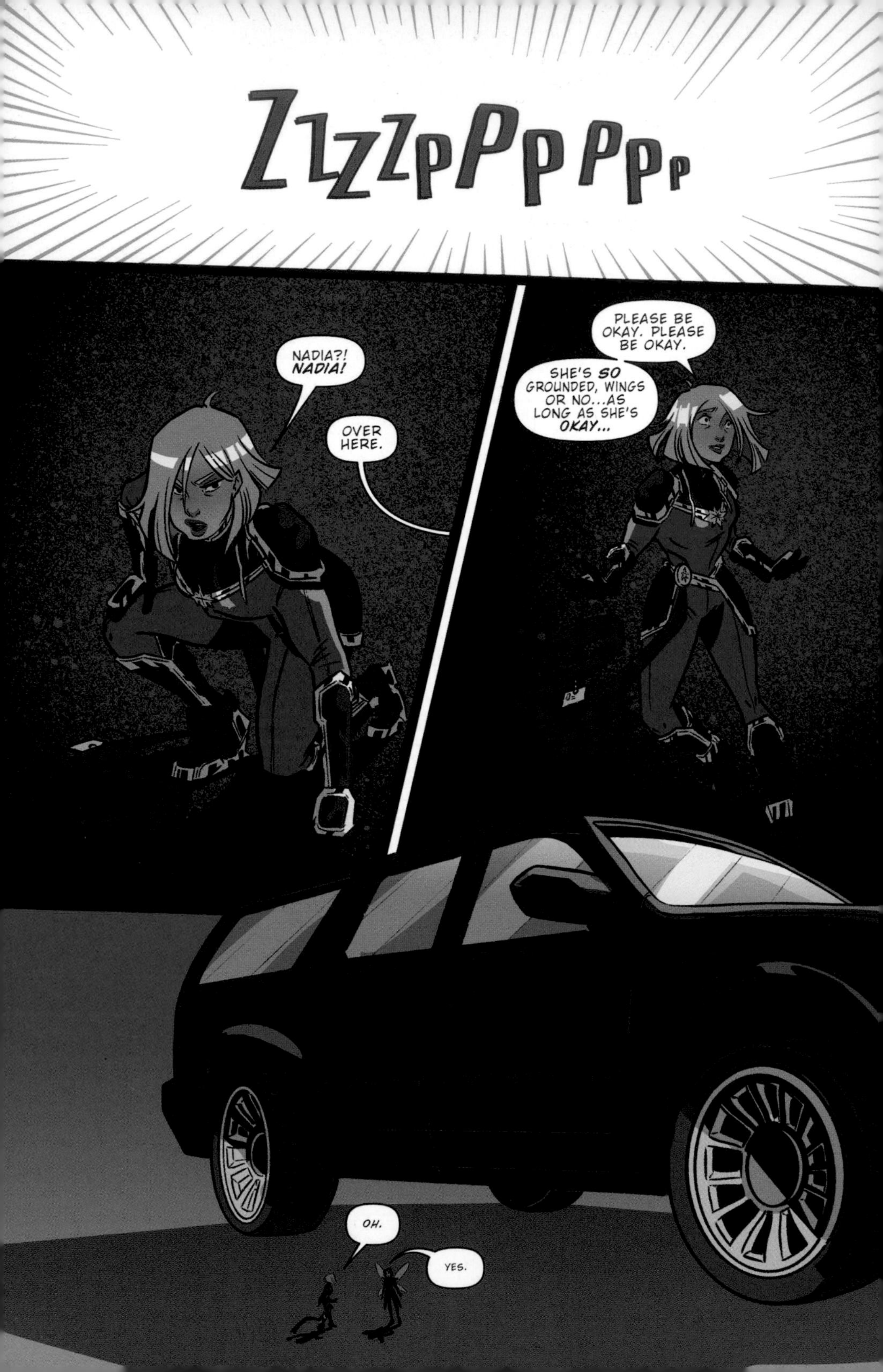
ZZZZZPPPPPPP
NADIA?! NADIA!
OVER HERE.
PLEASE BE OKAY. PLEASE BE OKAY.
SHE'S SO GROUNDED, WINGS OR NO...AS LONG AS SHE'S OKAY...
OH.
YES.

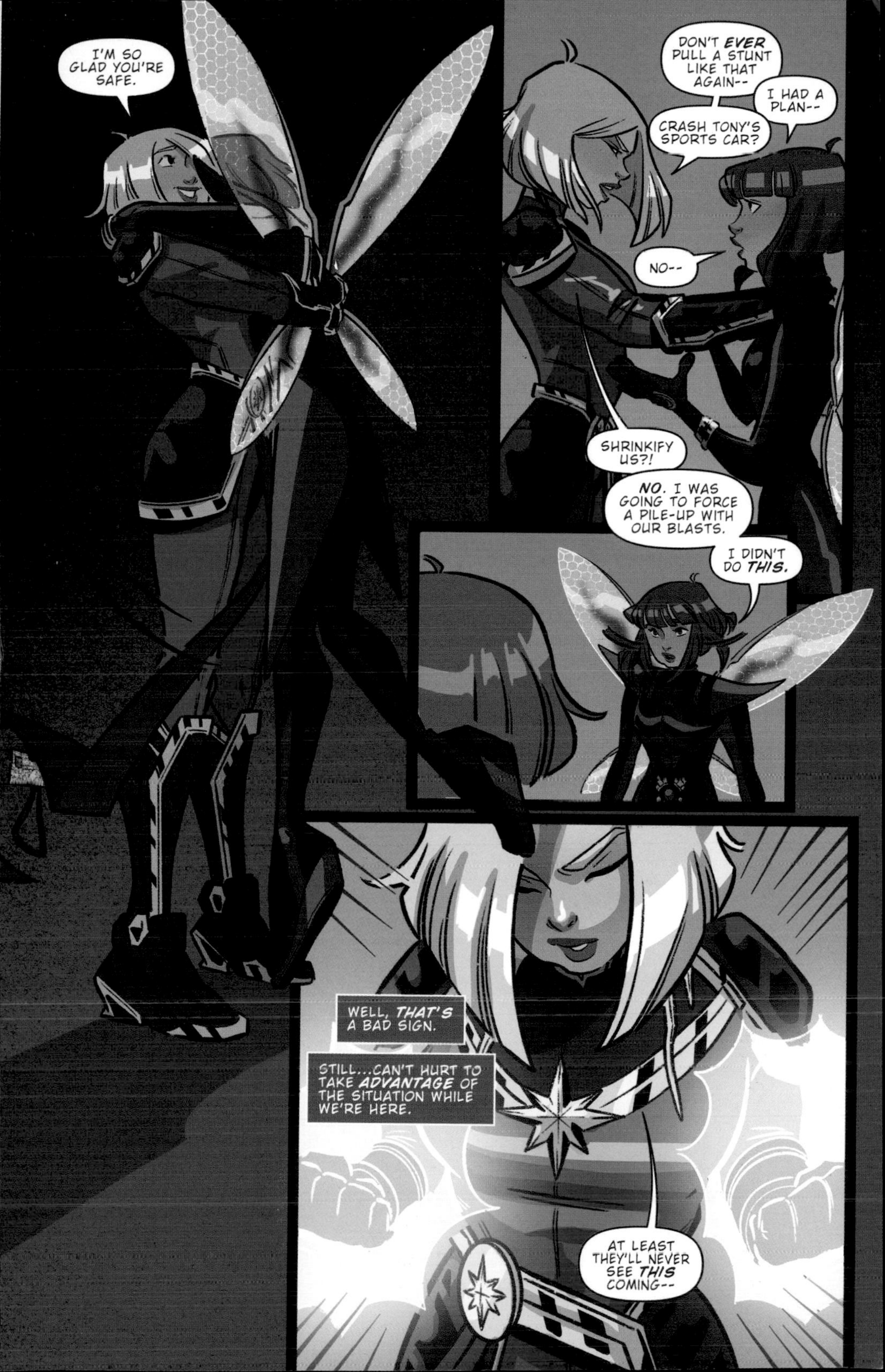
I'M SO GLAD YOU'RE SAFE.
DON'T EVER PULL A STUNT LIKE THAT AGAIN--
I HAD A PLAN--
CRASH TONY'S SPORTS CAR?
NO--
SHRINKIFY US?!
NO. I WAS GOING TO FORCE A PILE-UP WITH OUR BLASTS.
I DIDN'T DO THIS.
WELL, THAT'S A BAD SIGN.
STILL...CAN'T HURT TO TAKE ADVANTAGE OF THE SITUATION WHILE WE'RE HERE.
AT LEAST THEY'LL NEVER SEE THIS COMING--

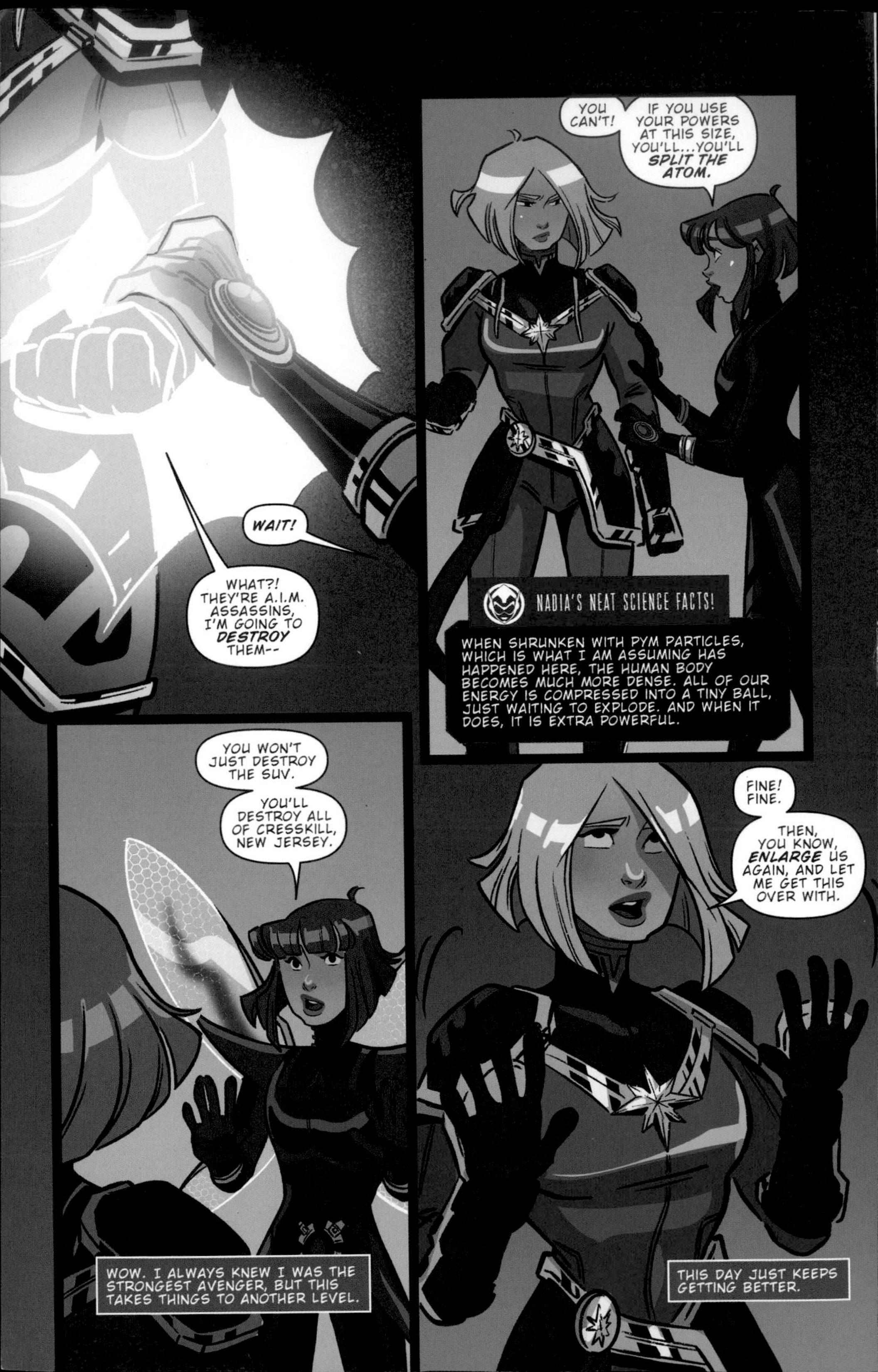
WAIT!
WHAT?! THEY'RE A.I.M. ASSASSINS, I'M GOING TO DESTROY THEM--
YOU CAN'T!
IF YOU USE YOUR POWERS AT THIS SIZE, YOU'LL...YOU'LL SPLIT THE ATOM.
NADIA'S NEAT SCIENCE FACTS!
WHEN SHRUNKEN WITH PYM PARTICLES, WHICH IS WHAT I AM ASSUMING HAS HAPPENED HERE, THE HUMAN BODY BECOMES MUCH MORE DENSE. ALL OF OUR ENERGY IS COMPRESSED INTO A TINY BALL, JUST WAITING TO EXPLODE. AND WHEN IT DOES, IT IS EXTRA POWERFUL.
YOU WON'T JUST DESTROY THE SUV.
YOU'LL DESTROY ALL OF CRESSKILL, NEW JERSEY.
WOW. I ALWAYS KNEW I WAS THE STRONGEST AVENGER, BUT THIS TAKES THINGS TO ANOTHER LEVEL.
FINE! FINE.
THEN, YOU KNOW, ENLARGE US AGAIN, AND LET ME GET THIS OVER WITH.
THIS DAY JUST KEEPS GETTING BETTER.

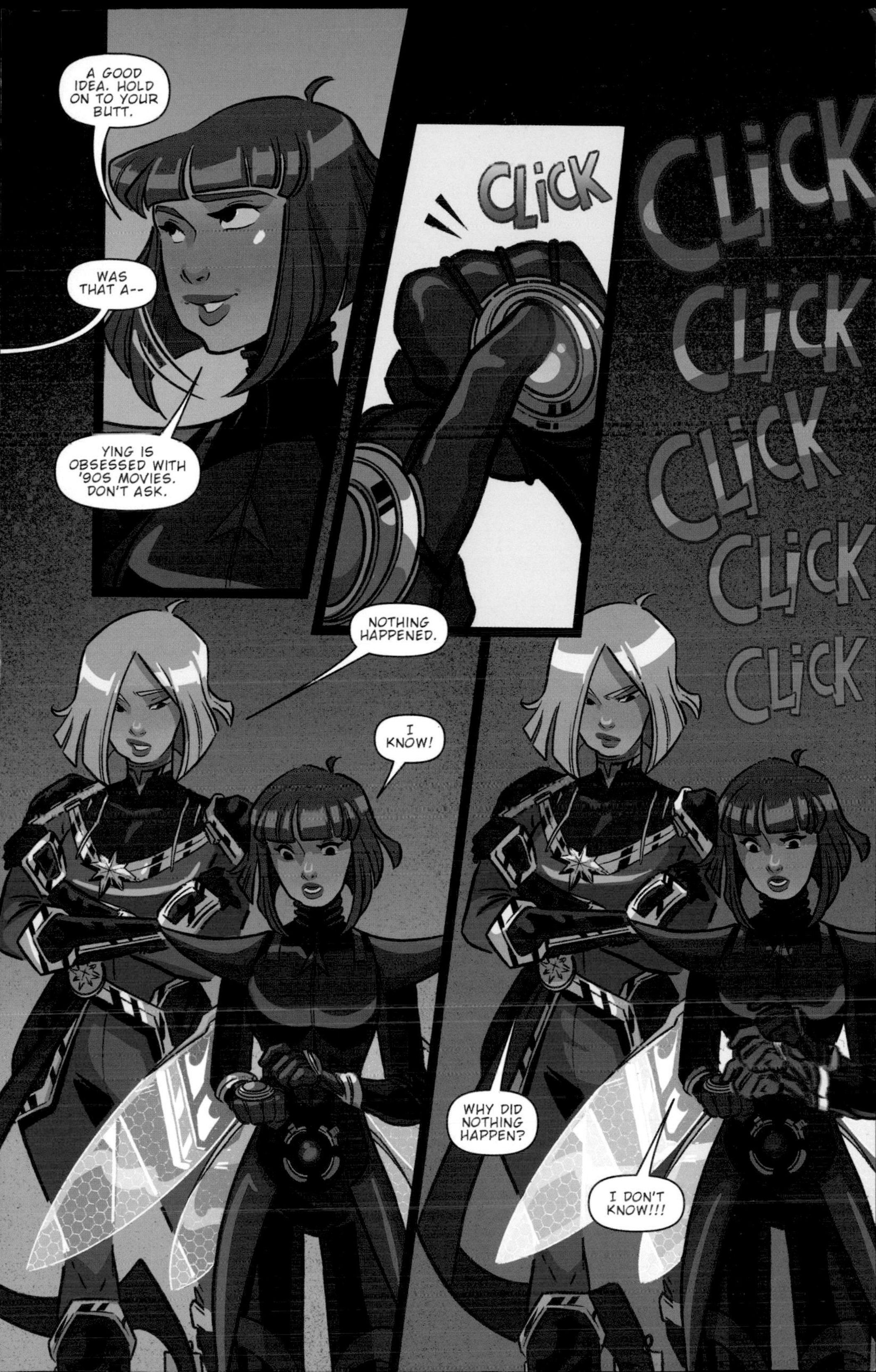
A GOOD IDEA. HOLD ON TO YOUR BUTT.
WAS THAT A--
YING IS OBSESSED WITH '90S MOVIES. DON'T ASK.
CLICK
CLICK
CLICK
CLICK
CLICK
CLICK
NOTHING HAPPENED.
I KNOW!
WHY DID NOTHING HAPPEN?
I DON'T KNOW!!!

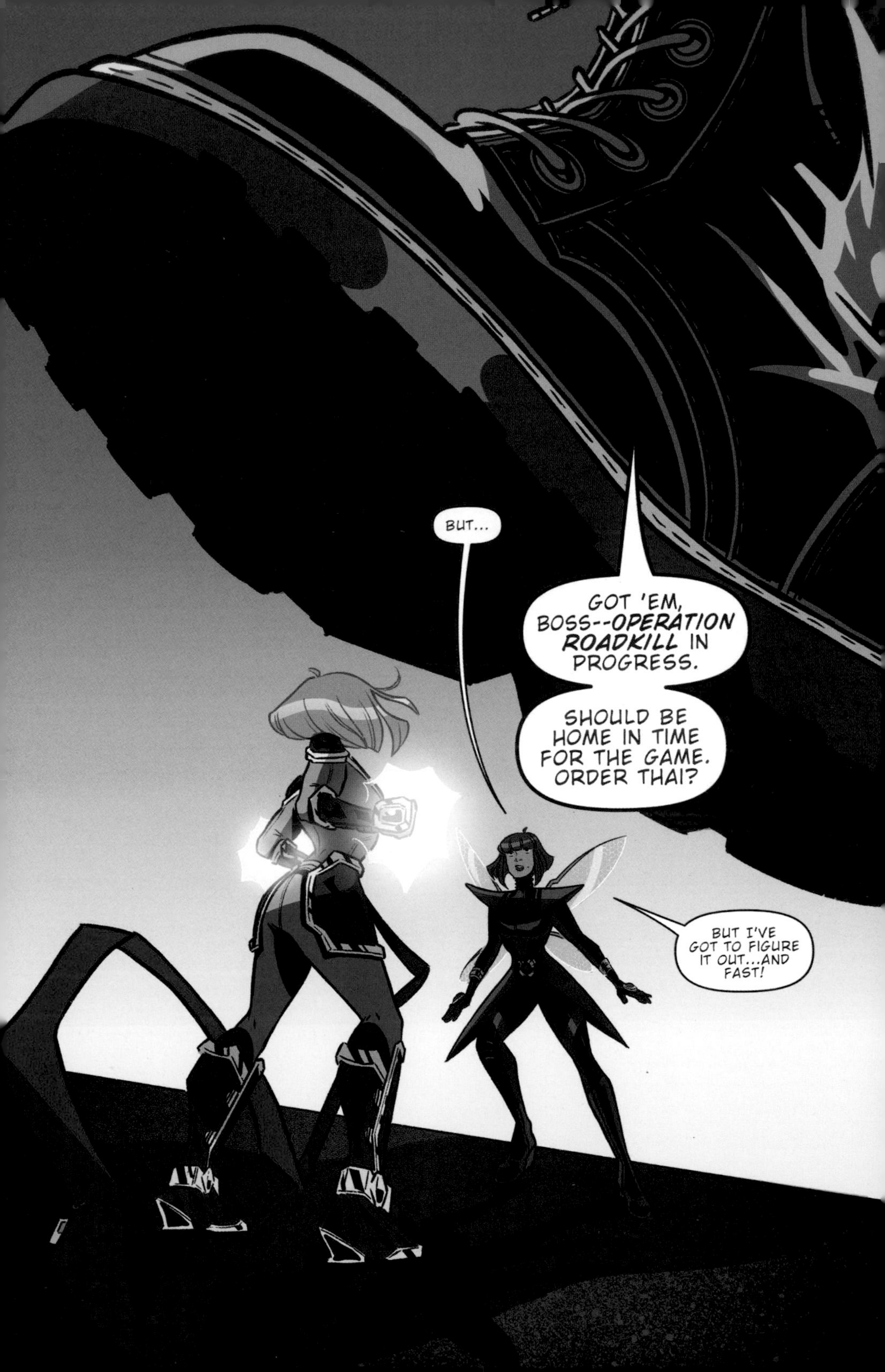
BUT...
GOT 'EM, BOSS--*OPERATION ROADKILL* IN PROGRESS.
SHOULD BE HOME IN TIME FOR THE GAME. ORDER THAI?
BUT I'VE GOT TO FIGURE IT OUT...AND FAST!

ART BY: **SWEENEY BOO**

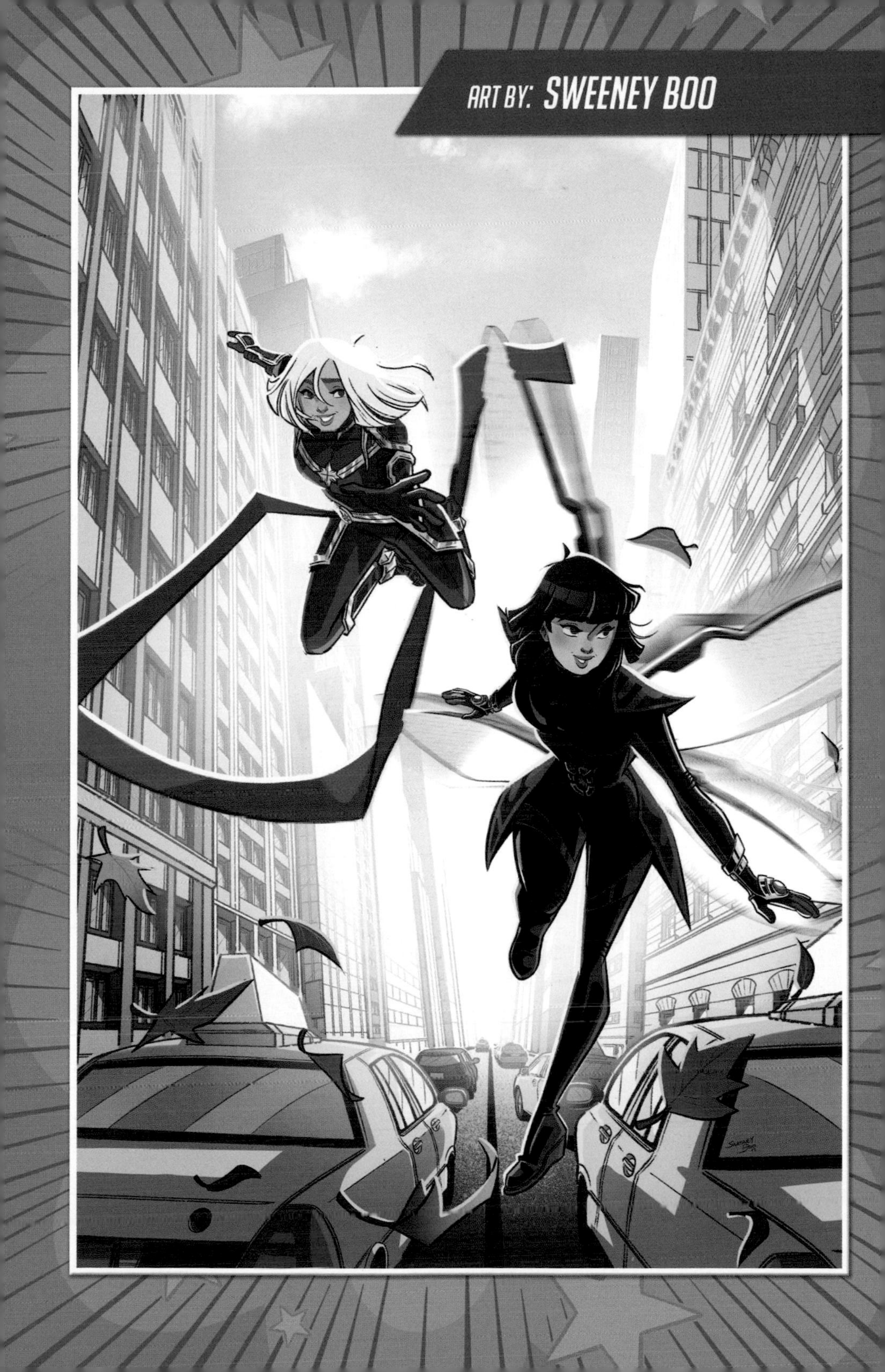

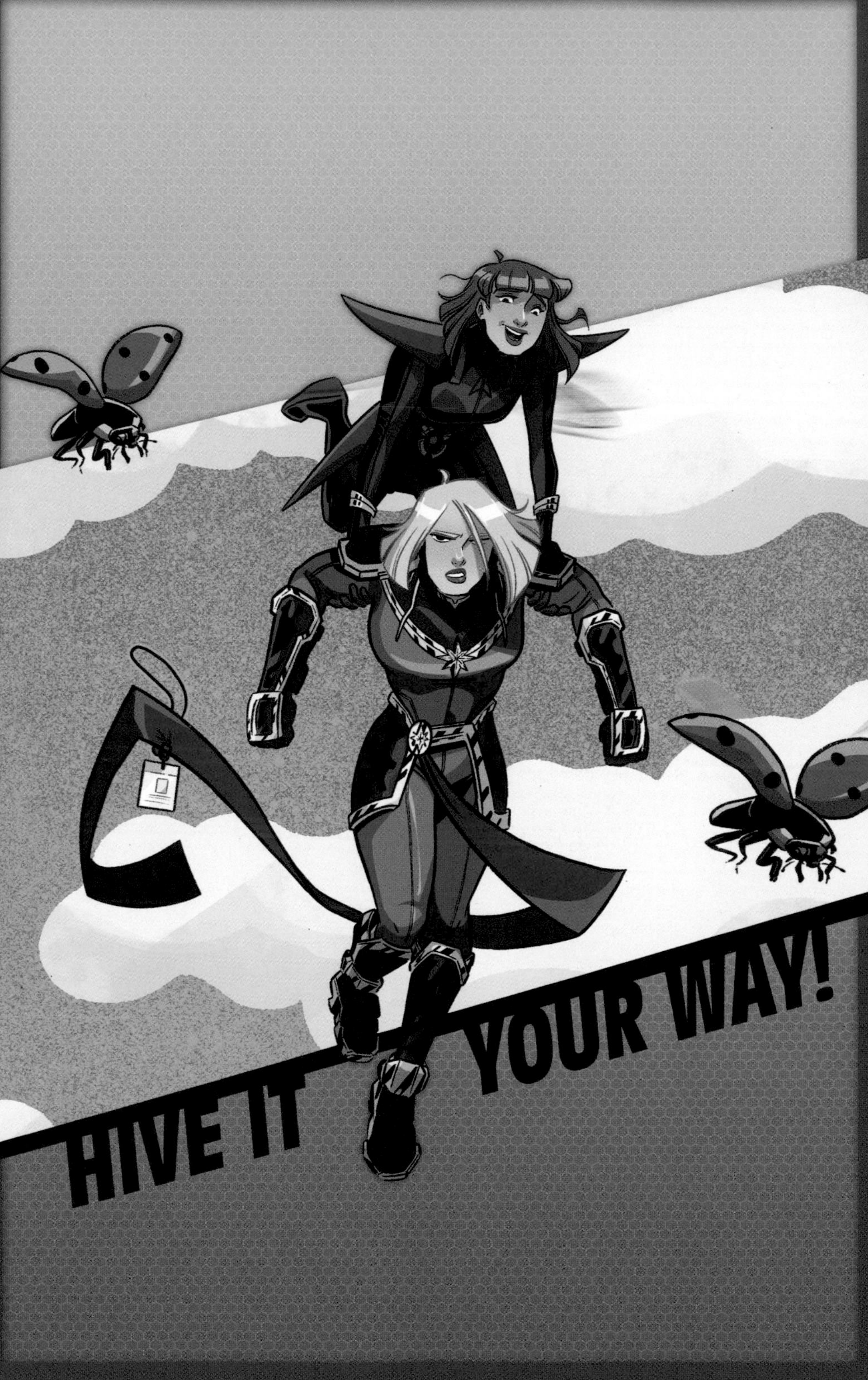
HIVE IT YOUR WAY!

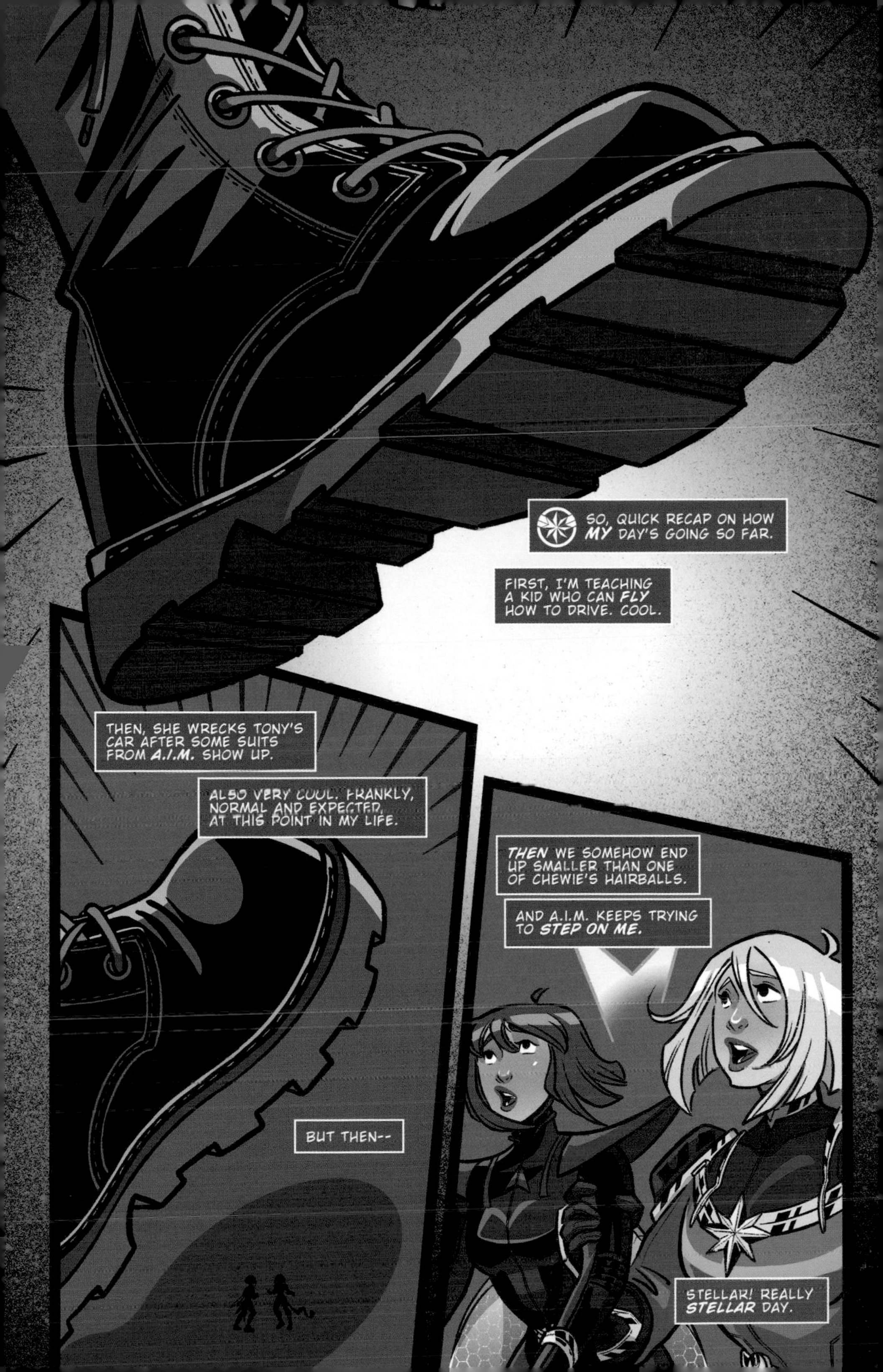
SO, QUICK RECAP ON HOW MY DAY'S GOING SO FAR.
FIRST, I'M TEACHING A KID WHO CAN FLY HOW TO DRIVE. COOL.
THEN, SHE WRECKS TONY'S CAR AFTER SOME SUITS FROM A.I.M. SHOW UP.
ALSO VERY COOL. FRANKLY, NORMAL AND EXPECTED, AT THIS POINT IN MY LIFE.
BUT THEN--
THEN WE SOMEHOW END UP SMALLER THAN ONE OF CHEWIE'S HAIRBALLS.
AND A.I.M. KEEPS TRYING TO STEP ON ME.
STELLAR! REALLY STELLAR DAY.

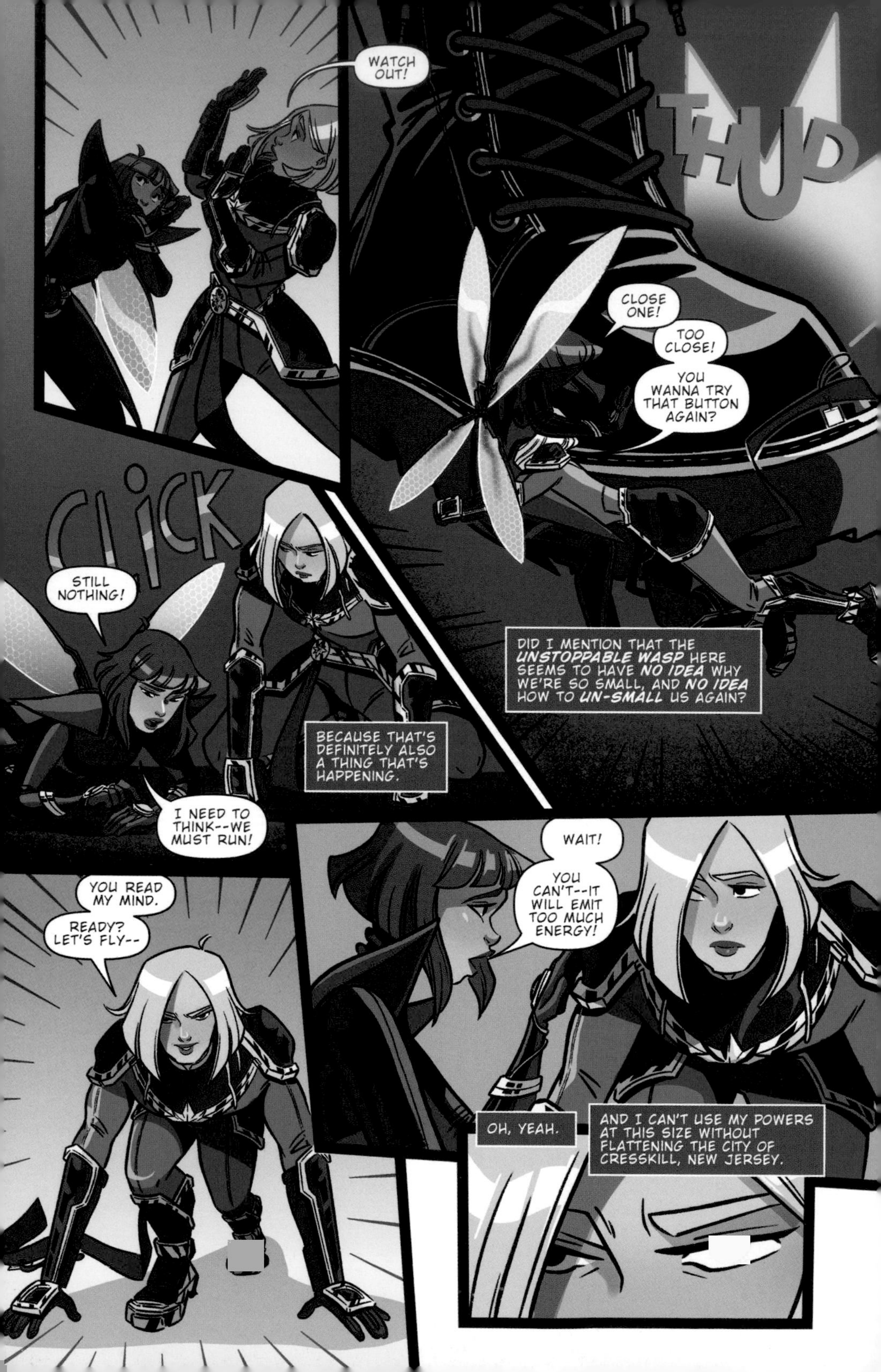
WATCH OUT!
THUD
CLOSE ONE!
TOO CLOSE!
YOU WANNA TRY THAT BUTTON AGAIN?
CLICK
STILL NOTHING!
BECAUSE THAT'S DEFINITELY ALSO A THING THAT'S HAPPENING.
I NEED TO THINK--WE MUST RUN!
DID I MENTION THAT THE UNSTOPPABLE WASP HERE SEEMS TO HAVE NO IDEA WHY WE'RE SO SMALL, AND NO IDEA HOW TO UN-SMALL US AGAIN?
YOU READ MY MIND.
READY? LET'S FLY--
WAIT!
YOU CAN'T--IT WILL EMIT TOO MUCH ENERGY!
OH, YEAH.
AND I CAN'T USE MY POWERS AT THIS SIZE WITHOUT FLATTENING THE CITY OF CRESSKILL, NEW JERSEY.

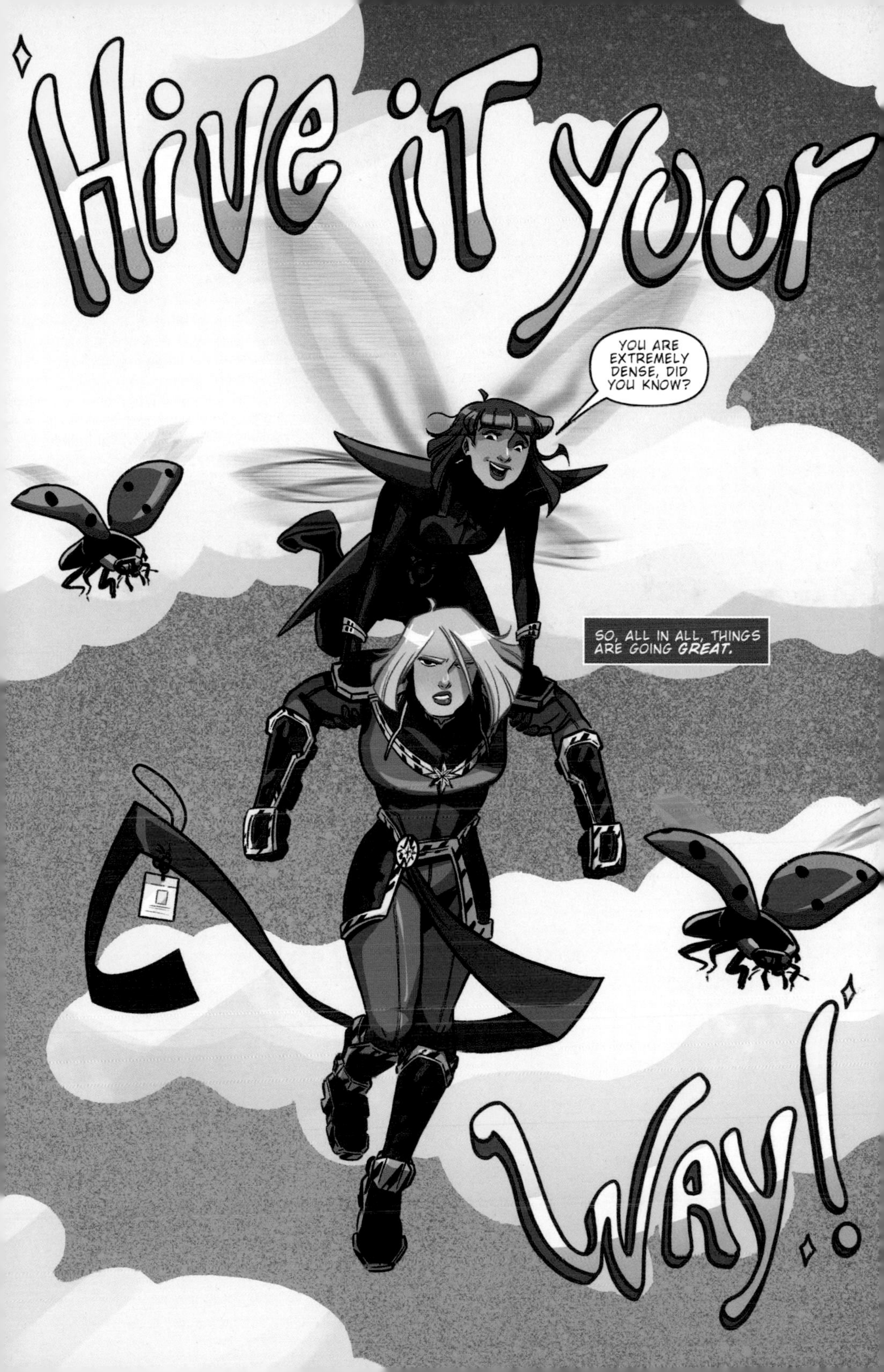
"Hive it your
You are extremely dense, did you know?
So, all in all, things are going *great.*
Way!"

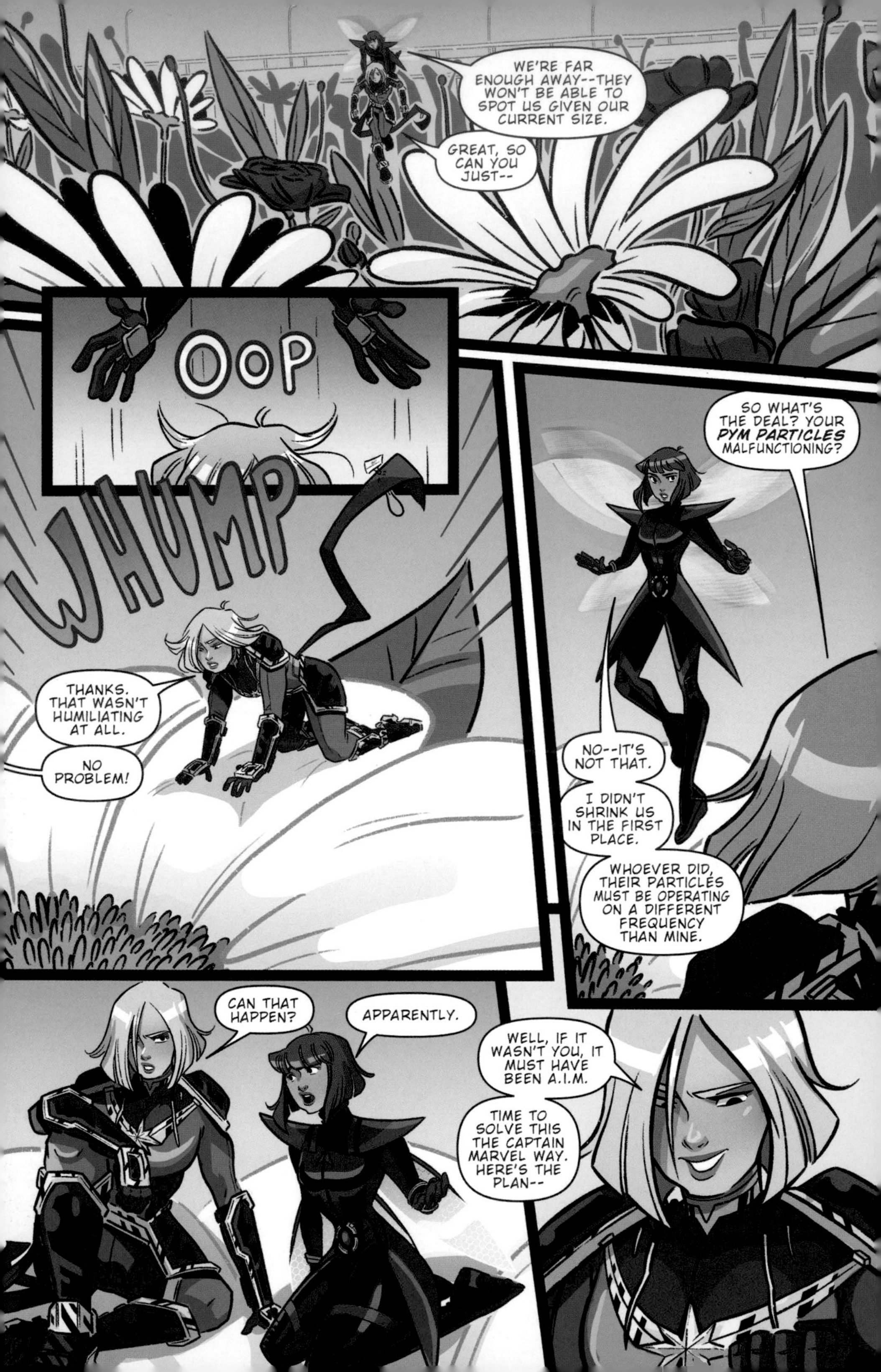
WE'RE FAR ENOUGH AWAY--THEY WON'T BE ABLE TO SPOT US GIVEN OUR CURRENT SIZE.
GREAT, SO CAN YOU JUST--
OOP
WHUMP
THANKS. THAT WASN'T HUMILIATING AT ALL.
NO PROBLEM!
SO WHAT'S THE DEAL? YOUR PYM PARTICLES MALFUNCTIONING?
NO--IT'S NOT THAT.
I DIDN'T SHRINK US IN THE FIRST PLACE.
WHOEVER DID, THEIR PARTICLES MUST BE OPERATING ON A DIFFERENT FREQUENCY THAN MINE.
CAN THAT HAPPEN?
APPARENTLY.
WELL, IF IT WASN'T YOU, IT MUST HAVE BEEN A.I.M.
TIME TO SOLVE THIS THE CAPTAIN MARVEL WAY. HERE'S THE PLAN--

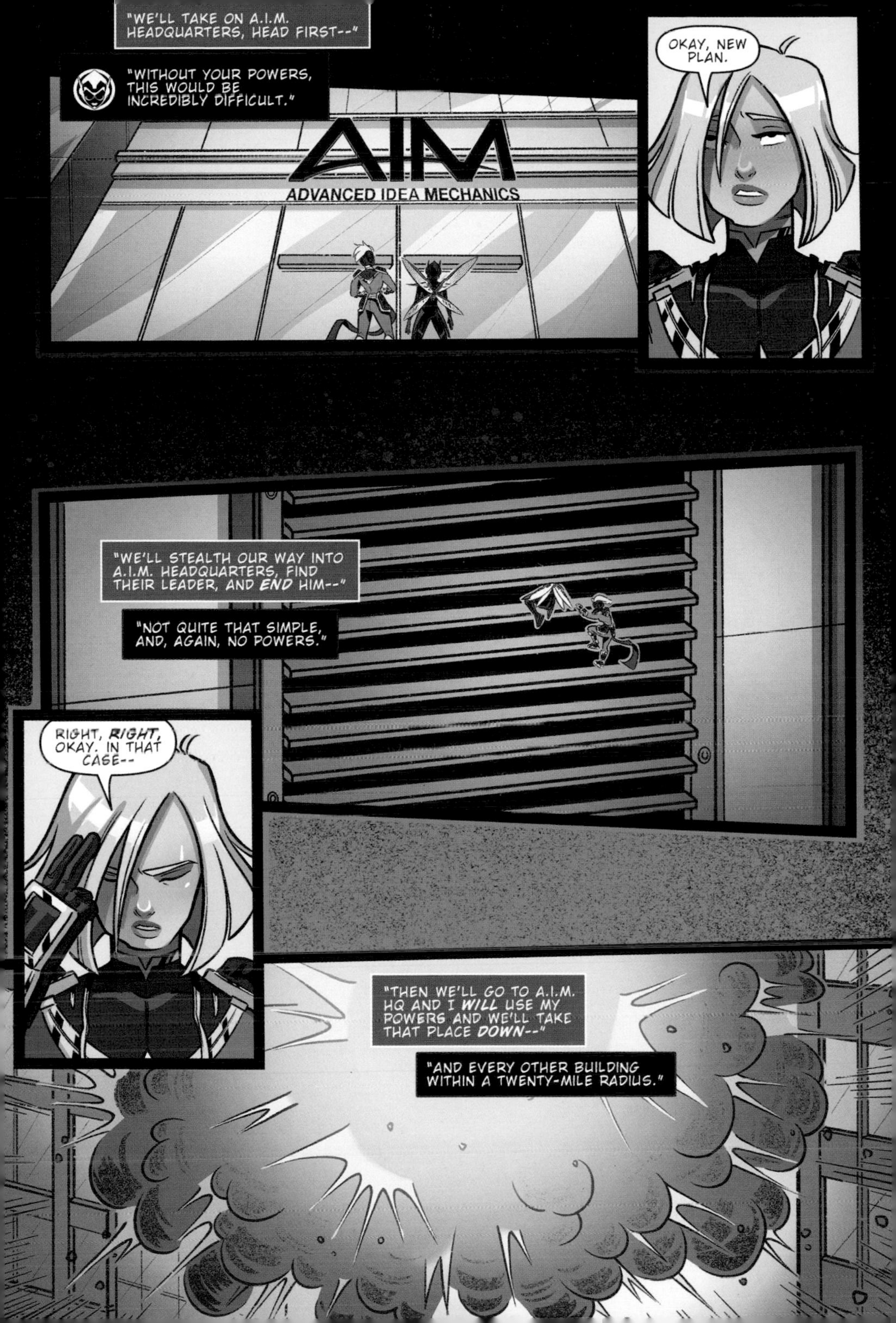
"WE'LL TAKE ON A.I.M. HEADQUARTERS, HEAD FIRST--"
"WITHOUT YOUR POWERS, THIS WOULD BE INCREDIBLY DIFFICULT."
AIM
ADVANCED IDEA MECHANICS
OKAY, NEW PLAN.
"WE'LL STEALTH OUR WAY INTO A.I.M. HEADQUARTERS, FIND THEIR LEADER, AND *END* HIM--"
"NOT QUITE THAT SIMPLE, AND, AGAIN, NO POWERS."
RIGHT, ***RIGHT***, OKAY. IN THAT CASE--
"THEN WE'LL GO TO A.I.M. HQ AND I ***WILL*** USE MY POWERS AND WE'LL TAKE THAT PLACE *DOWN*--"
"AND EVERY OTHER BUILDING WITHIN A TWENTY-MILE RADIUS."

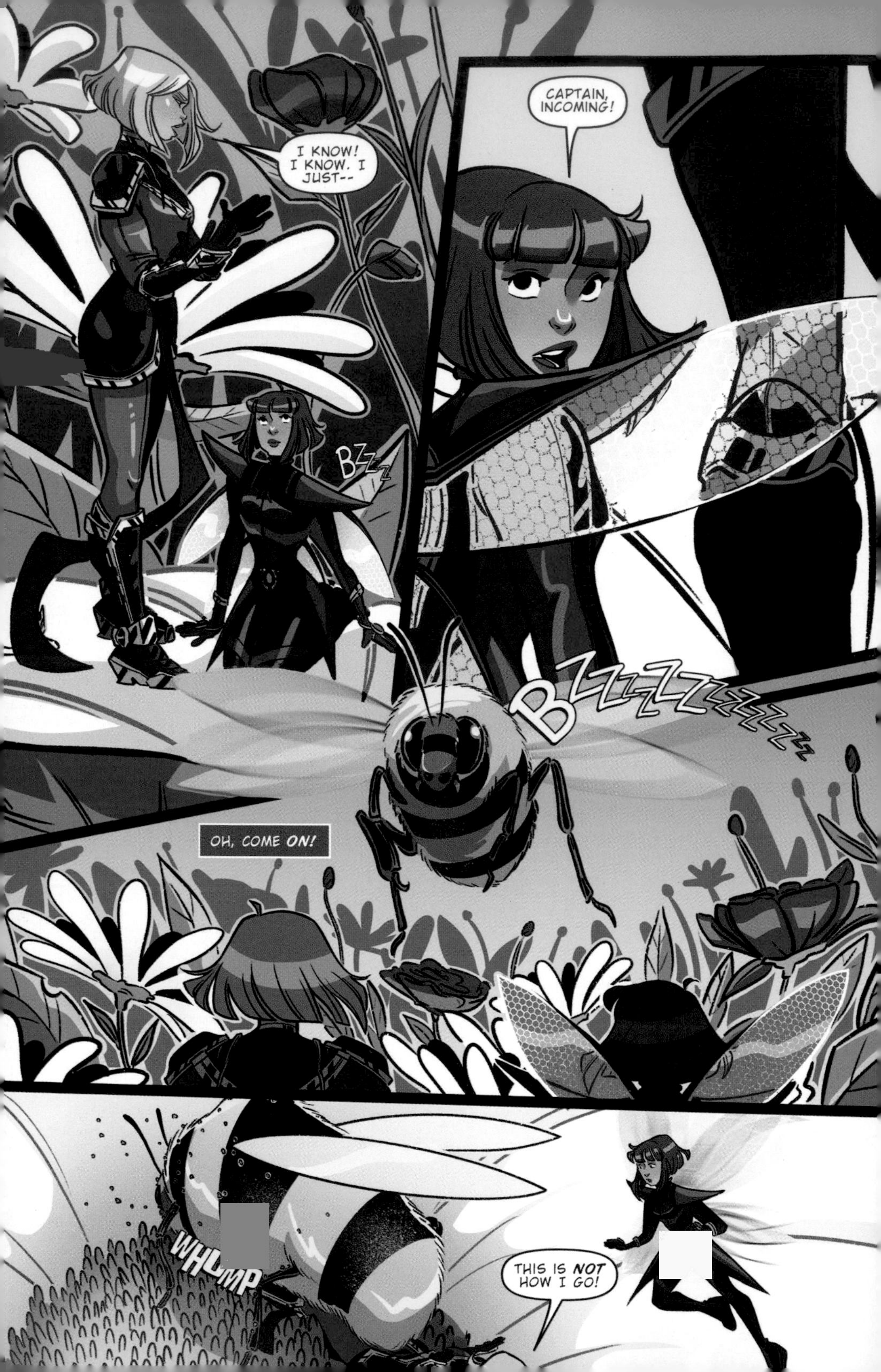
I KNOW! I KNOW. I JUST--
BZZZ
CAPTAIN, INCOMING!
BZZZZZZZZZZZZZZ
OH, COME ON!
WHUMP
THIS IS NOT HOW I GO!

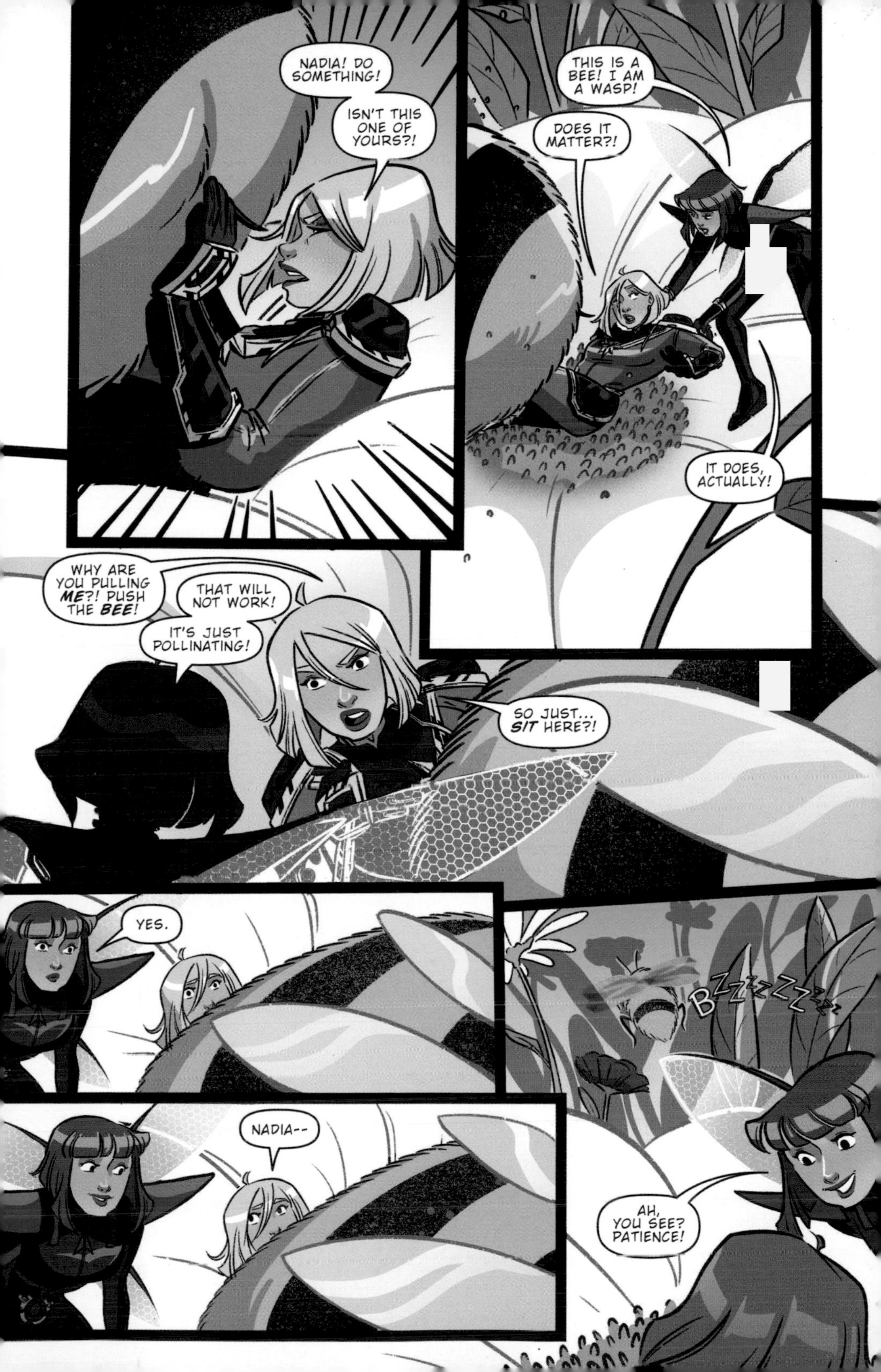
NADIA! DO SOMETHING!
ISN'T THIS ONE OF YOURS?!
THIS IS A BEE! I AM A WASP!
DOES IT MATTER?!
IT DOES, ACTUALLY!
WHY ARE YOU PULLING ME?! PUSH THE BEE!
THAT WILL NOT WORK!
IT'S JUST POLLINATING!
SO JUST... SIT HERE?!
YES.
BZZZZZZZZZ
NADIA--
AH, YOU SEE? PATIENCE!

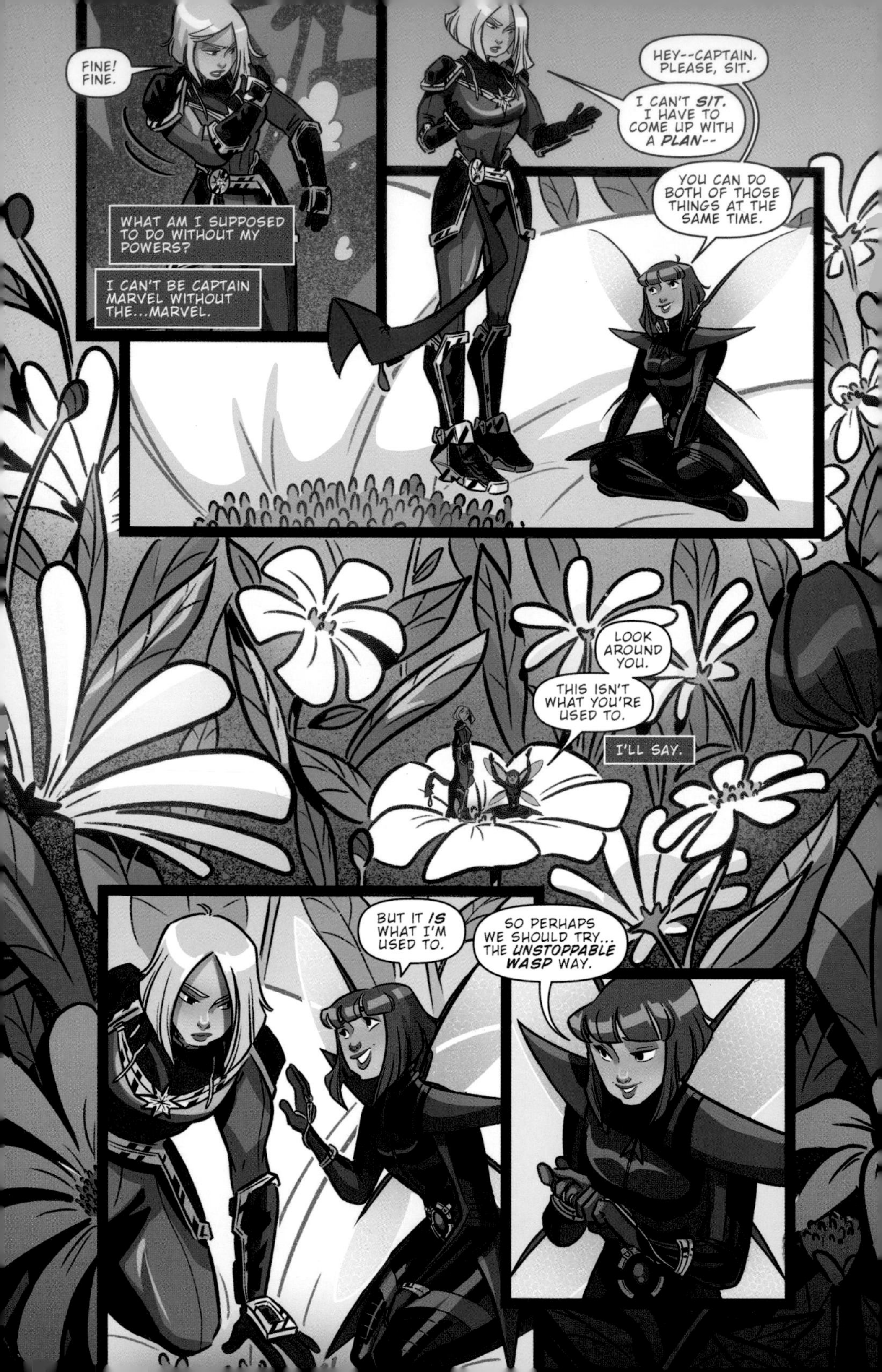
FINE! FINE.
WHAT AM I SUPPOSED TO DO WITHOUT MY POWERS?
I CAN'T BE CAPTAIN MARVEL WITHOUT THE...MARVEL.
HEY--CAPTAIN. PLEASE, SIT.
I CAN'T SIT. I HAVE TO COME UP WITH A PLAN--
YOU CAN DO BOTH OF THOSE THINGS AT THE SAME TIME.
LOOK AROUND YOU.
THIS ISN'T WHAT YOU'RE USED TO.
I'LL SAY.
BUT IT IS WHAT I'M USED TO.
SO PERHAPS WE SHOULD TRY... THE UNSTOPPABLE WASP WAY.

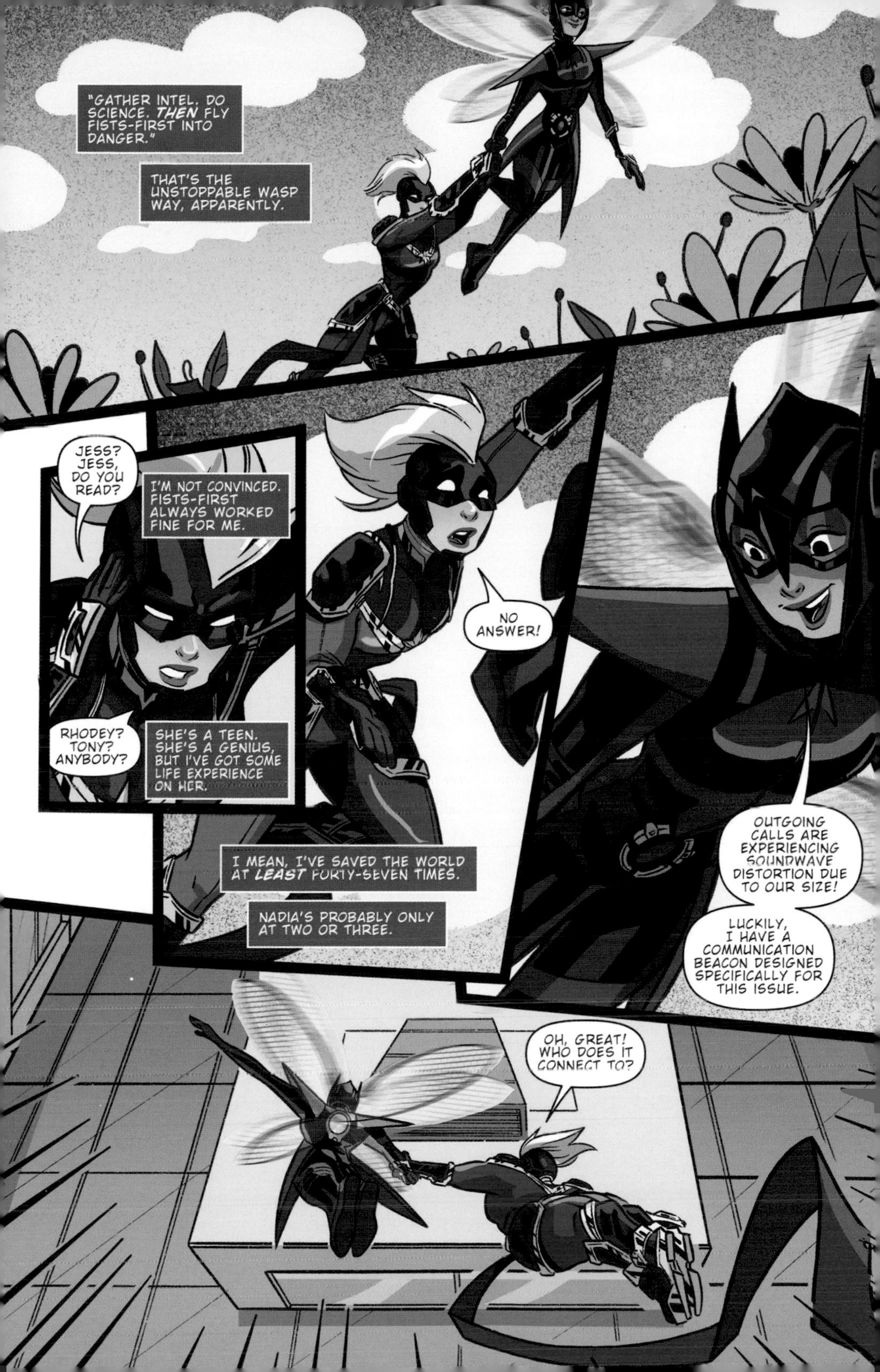
"GATHER INTEL. DO SCIENCE. THEN FLY FISTS-FIRST INTO DANGER."
THAT'S THE UNSTOPPABLE WASP WAY, APPARENTLY.
JESS? JESS, DO YOU READ?
I'M NOT CONVINCED. FISTS-FIRST ALWAYS WORKED FINE FOR ME.
RHODEY? TONY? ANYBODY?
SHE'S A TEEN. SHE'S A GENIUS, BUT I'VE GOT SOME LIFE EXPERIENCE ON HER.
NO ANSWER!
I MEAN, I'VE SAVED THE WORLD AT LEAST FORTY-SEVEN TIMES.
NADIA'S PROBABLY ONLY AT TWO OR THREE.
OUTGOING CALLS ARE EXPERIENCING SOUNDWAVE DISTORTION DUE TO OUR SIZE!
LUCKILY, I HAVE A COMMUNICATION BEACON DESIGNED SPECIFICALLY FOR THIS ISSUE.
OH, GREAT! WHO DOES IT CONNECT TO?

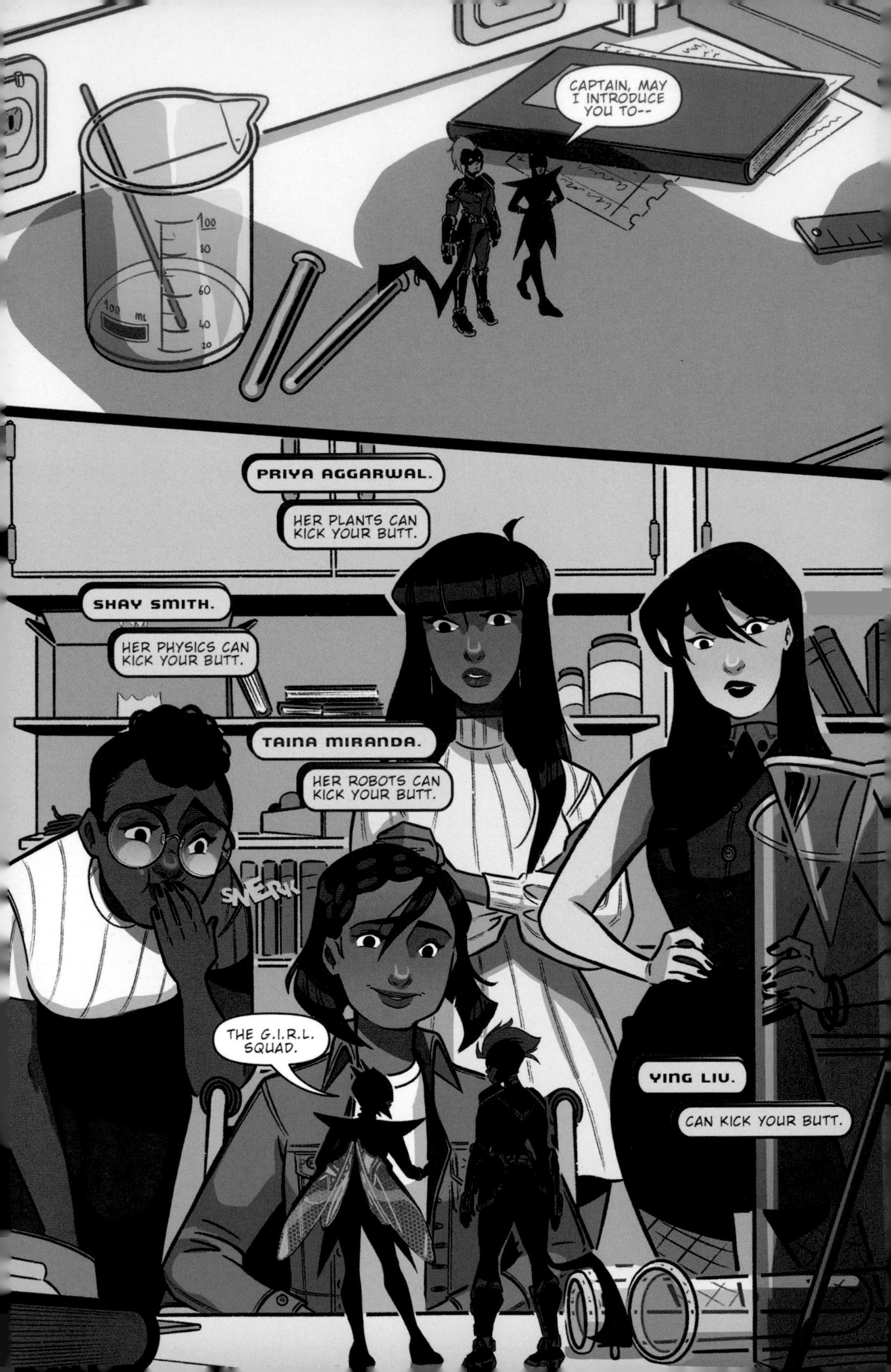
CAPTAIN, MAY I INTRODUCE YOU TO--
PRIYA AGGARWAL.
HER PLANTS CAN KICK YOUR BUTT.
SHAY SMITH.
HER PHYSICS CAN KICK YOUR BUTT.
TAINA MIRANDA.
HER ROBOTS CAN KICK YOUR BUTT.
SNERK
THE G.I.R.L. SQUAD.
YING LIU.
CAN KICK YOUR BUTT.

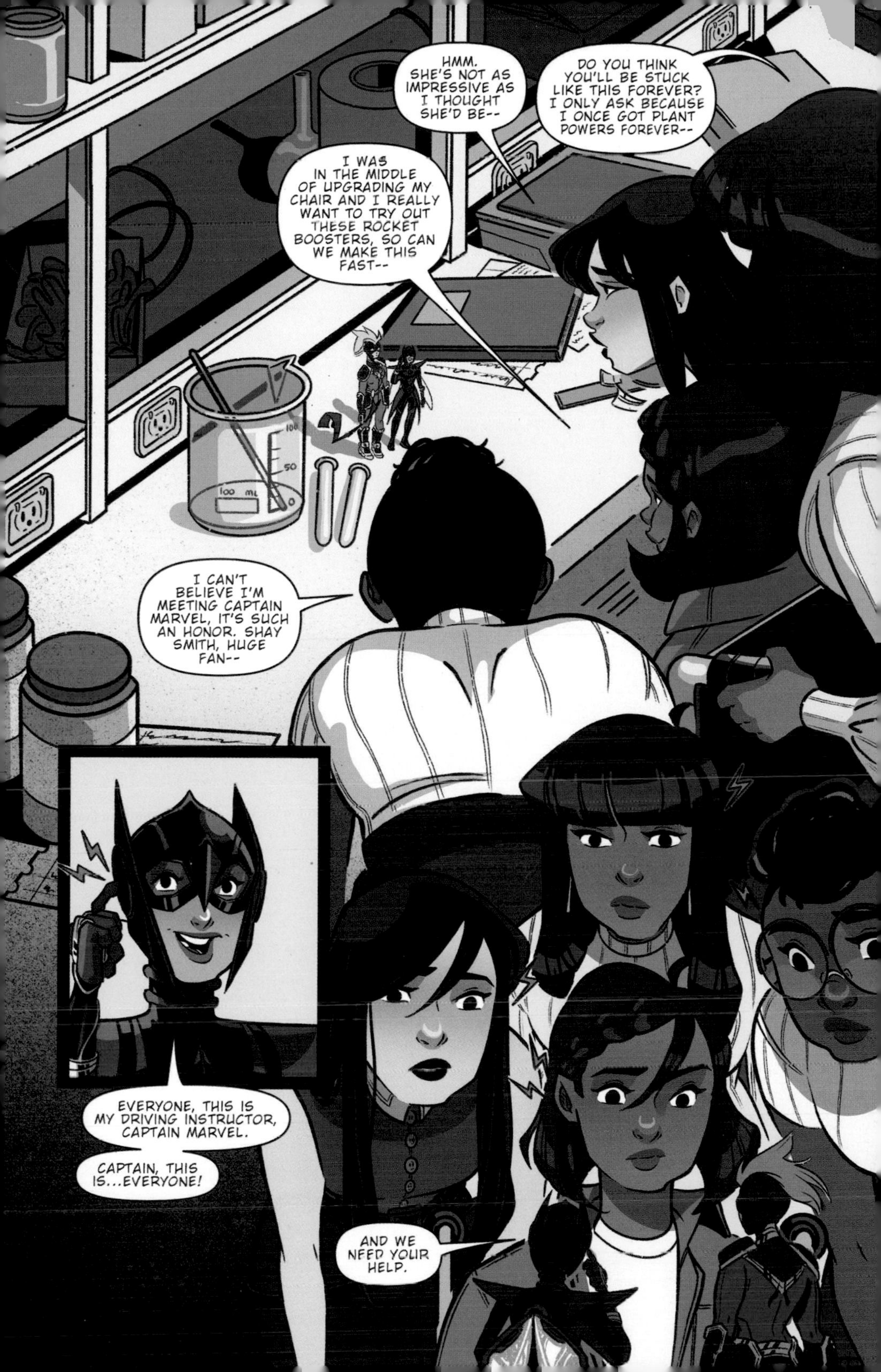
HMM. SHE'S NOT AS IMPRESSIVE AS I THOUGHT SHE'D BE--
DO YOU THINK YOU'LL BE STUCK LIKE THIS FOREVER? I ONLY ASK BECAUSE I ONCE GOT PLANT POWERS FOREVER--
I WAS IN THE MIDDLE OF UPGRADING MY CHAIR AND I REALLY WANT TO TRY OUT THESE ROCKET BOOSTERS, SO CAN WE MAKE THIS FAST--
I CAN'T BELIEVE I'M MEETING CAPTAIN MARVEL, IT'S SUCH AN HONOR. SHAY SMITH, HUGE FAN--
EVERYONE, THIS IS MY DRIVING INSTRUCTOR, CAPTAIN MARVEL.
CAPTAIN, THIS IS...EVERYONE!
AND WE NEED YOUR HELP.

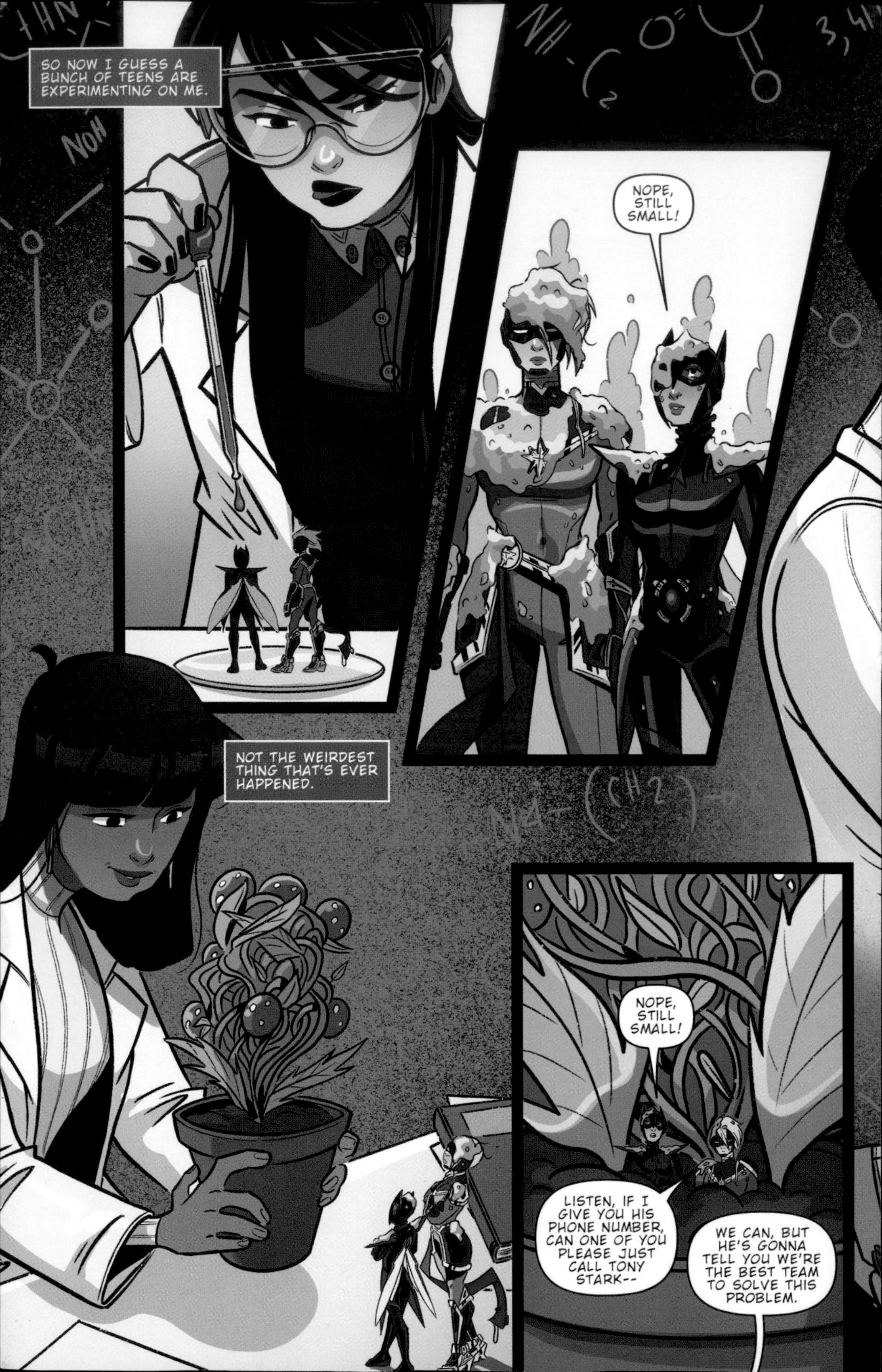
SO NOW I GUESS A BUNCH OF TEENS ARE EXPERIMENTING ON ME.
NOPE, STILL SMALL!
NOT THE WEIRDEST THING THAT'S EVER HAPPENED.
NOPE, STILL SMALL!
LISTEN, IF I GIVE YOU HIS PHONE NUMBER, CAN ONE OF YOU PLEASE JUST CALL TONY STARK--
WE CAN, BUT HE'S GONNA TELL YOU WE'RE THE BEST TEAM TO SOLVE THIS PROBLEM.

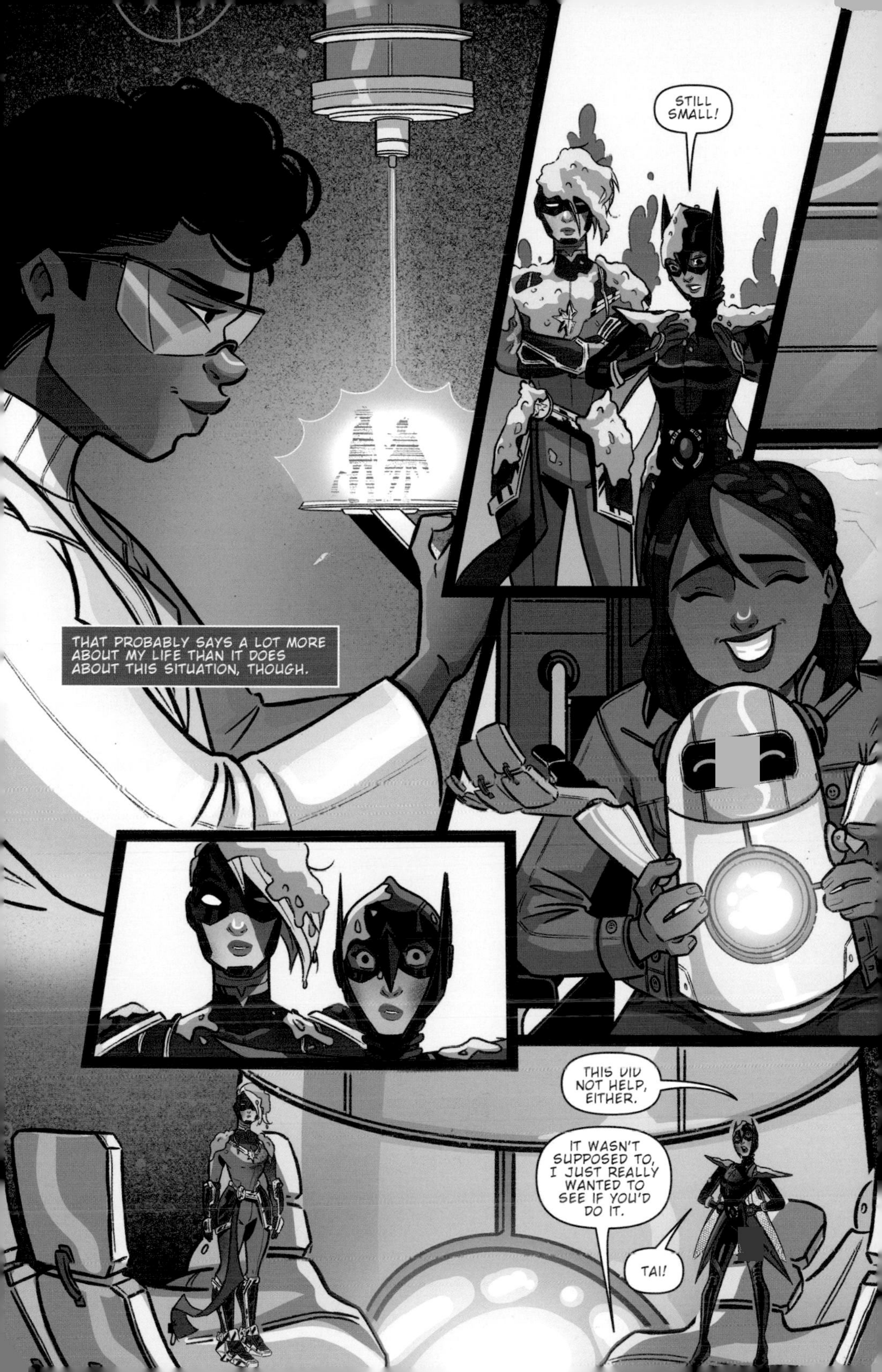

THAT PROBABLY SAYS A LOT MORE ABOUT MY LIFE THAN IT DOES ABOUT THIS SITUATION, THOUGH.
STILL SMALL!
THIS DID NOT HELP, EITHER.
IT WASN'T SUPPOSED TO, I JUST REALLY WANTED TO SEE IF YOU'D DO IT.
TAI!

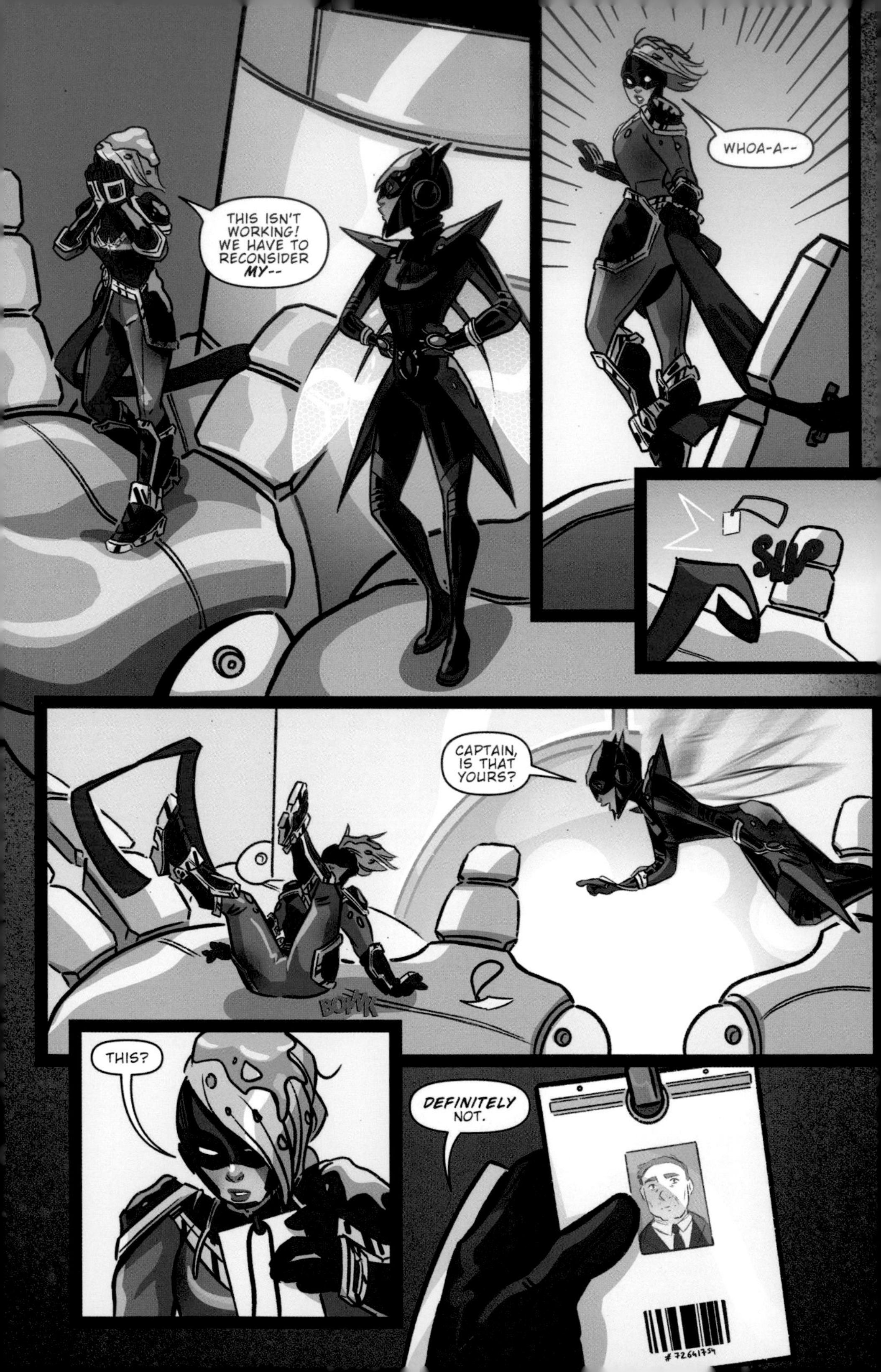

THIS ISN'T WORKING! WE HAVE TO RECONSIDER MY--
WHOA-A--
SLIP
CAPTAIN, IS THAT YOURS?
BONK
THIS?
DEFINITELY NOT.
#72641754

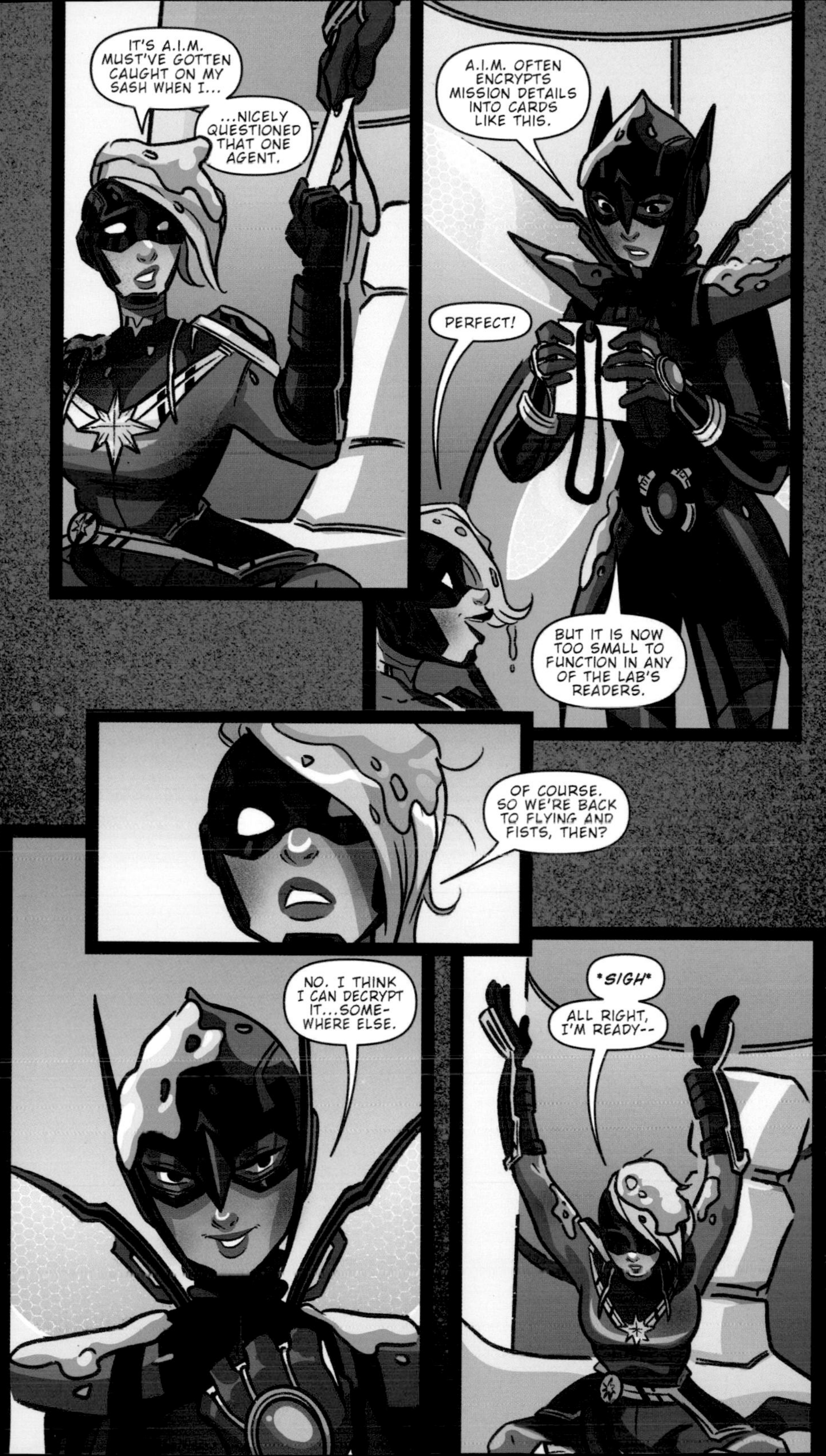

IT'S A.I.M. MUST'VE GOTTEN CAUGHT ON MY SASH WHEN I...
...NICELY QUESTIONED THAT ONE AGENT.
A.I.M. OFTEN ENCRYPTS MISSION DETAILS INTO CARDS LIKE THIS.
PERFECT!
BUT IT IS NOW TOO SMALL TO FUNCTION IN ANY OF THE LAB'S READERS.
OF COURSE. SO WE'RE BACK TO FLYING AND FISTS, THEN?
NO. I THINK I CAN DECRYPT IT...SOME-WHERE ELSE.
SIGH
ALL RIGHT, I'M READY--

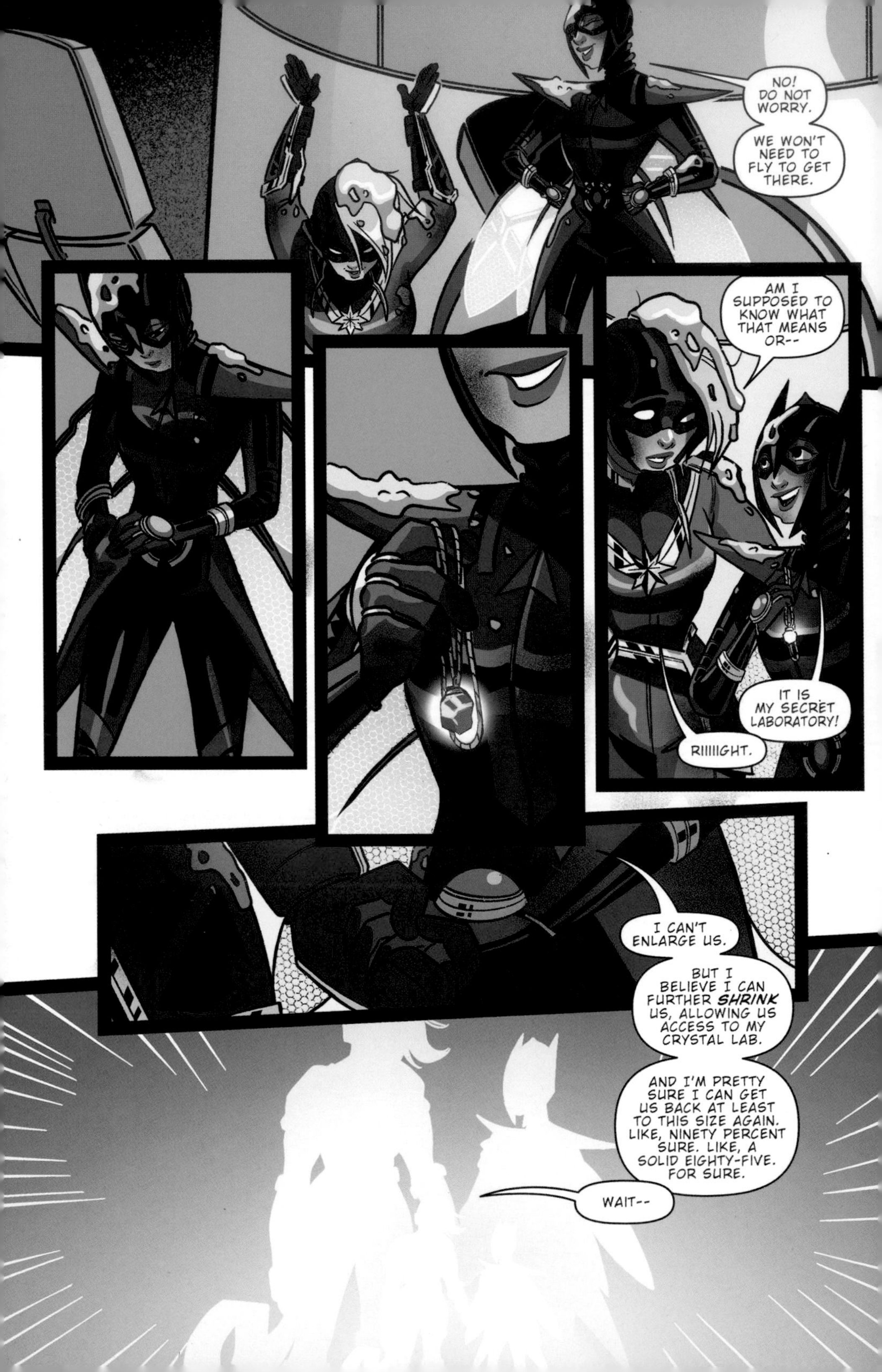
NO! DO NOT WORRY.
WE WON'T NEED TO FLY TO GET THERE.
AM I SUPPOSED TO KNOW WHAT THAT MEANS OR--
IT IS MY SECRET LABORATORY!
RIIIIIGHT.
I CAN'T ENLARGE US.
BUT I BELIEVE I CAN FURTHER SHRINK US, ALLOWING US ACCESS TO MY CRYSTAL LAB.
AND I'M PRETTY SURE I CAN GET US BACK AT LEAST TO THIS SIZE AGAIN. LIKE, NINETY PERCENT SURE. LIKE, A SOLID EIGHTY-FIVE. FOR SURE.
WAIT--

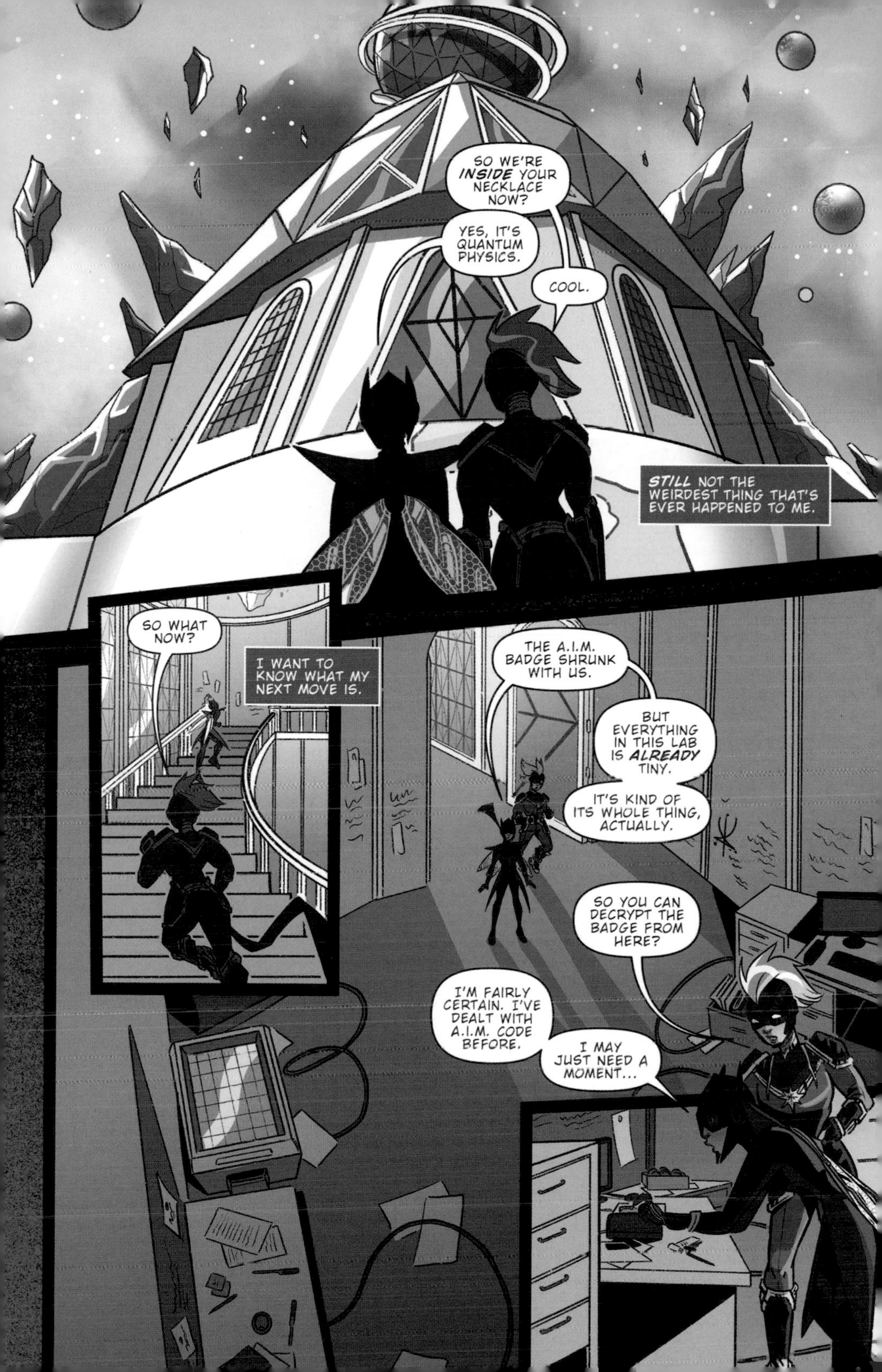
SO WE'RE INSIDE YOUR NECKLACE NOW?
YES, IT'S QUANTUM PHYSICS.
COOL.
STILL NOT THE WEIRDEST THING THAT'S EVER HAPPENED TO ME.
SO WHAT NOW?
I WANT TO KNOW WHAT MY NEXT MOVE IS.
THE A.I.M. BADGE SHRUNK WITH US.
BUT EVERYTHING IN THIS LAB IS ALREADY TINY.
IT'S KIND OF ITS WHOLE THING, ACTUALLY.
SO YOU CAN DECRYPT THE BADGE FROM HERE?
I'M FAIRLY CERTAIN. I'VE DEALT WITH A.I.M. CODE BEFORE.
I MAY JUST NEED A MOMENT...

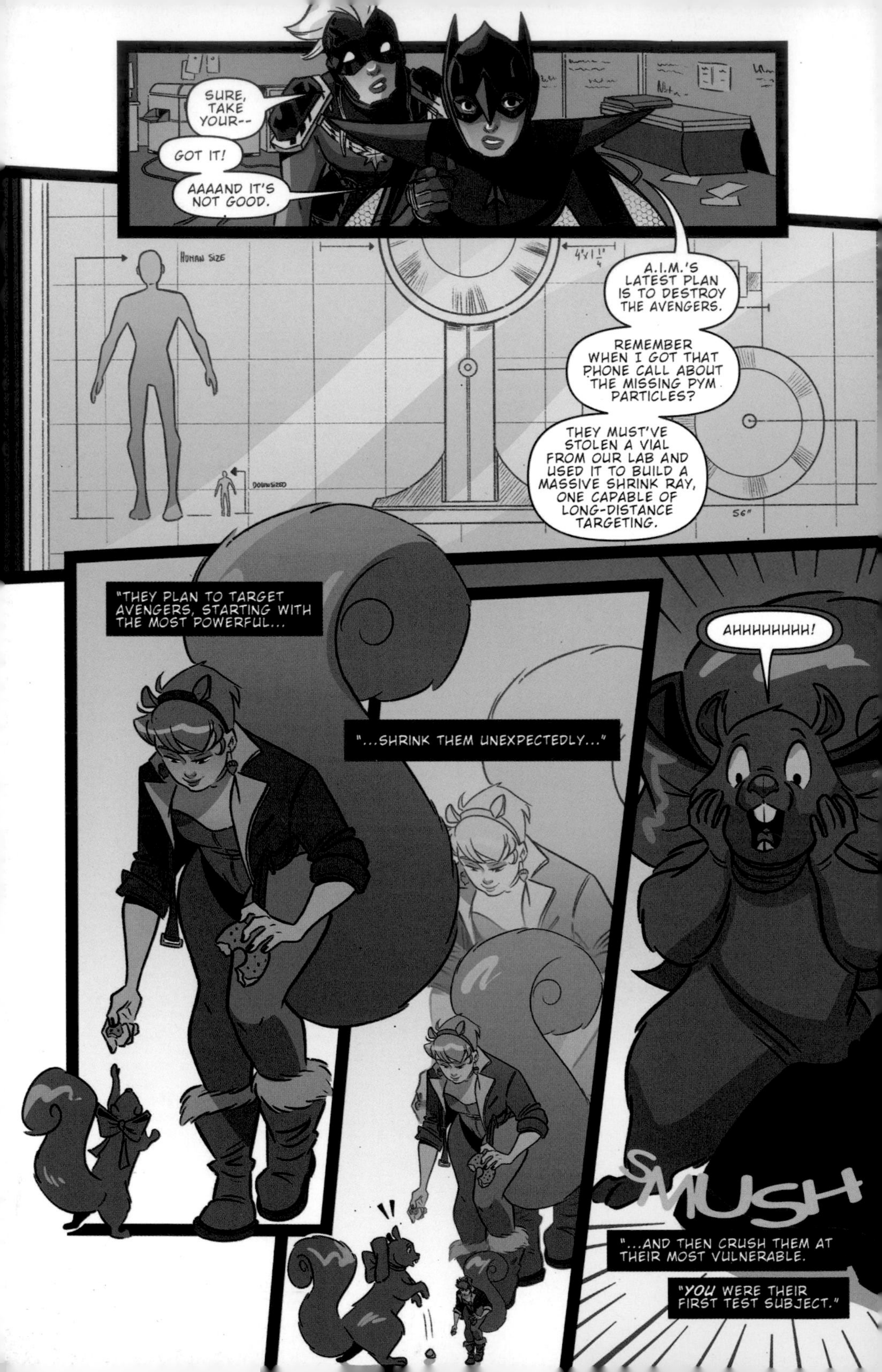
SURE, TAKE YOUR--
GOT IT!
AAAAND IT'S NOT GOOD.
HUMAN SIZE
DOWNSIZED
A.I.M.'S LATEST PLAN IS TO DESTROY THE AVENGERS.
REMEMBER WHEN I GOT THAT PHONE CALL ABOUT THE MISSING PYM PARTICLES?
THEY MUST'VE STOLEN A VIAL FROM OUR LAB AND USED IT TO BUILD A MASSIVE SHRINK RAY, ONE CAPABLE OF LONG-DISTANCE TARGETING.
"THEY PLAN TO TARGET AVENGERS, STARTING WITH THE MOST POWERFUL...
"...SHRINK THEM UNEXPECTEDLY..."
!!
AHHHHHHHH!
SMUSH
"...AND THEN CRUSH THEM AT THEIR MOST VULNERABLE.
"YOU WERE THEIR FIRST TEST SUBJECT."

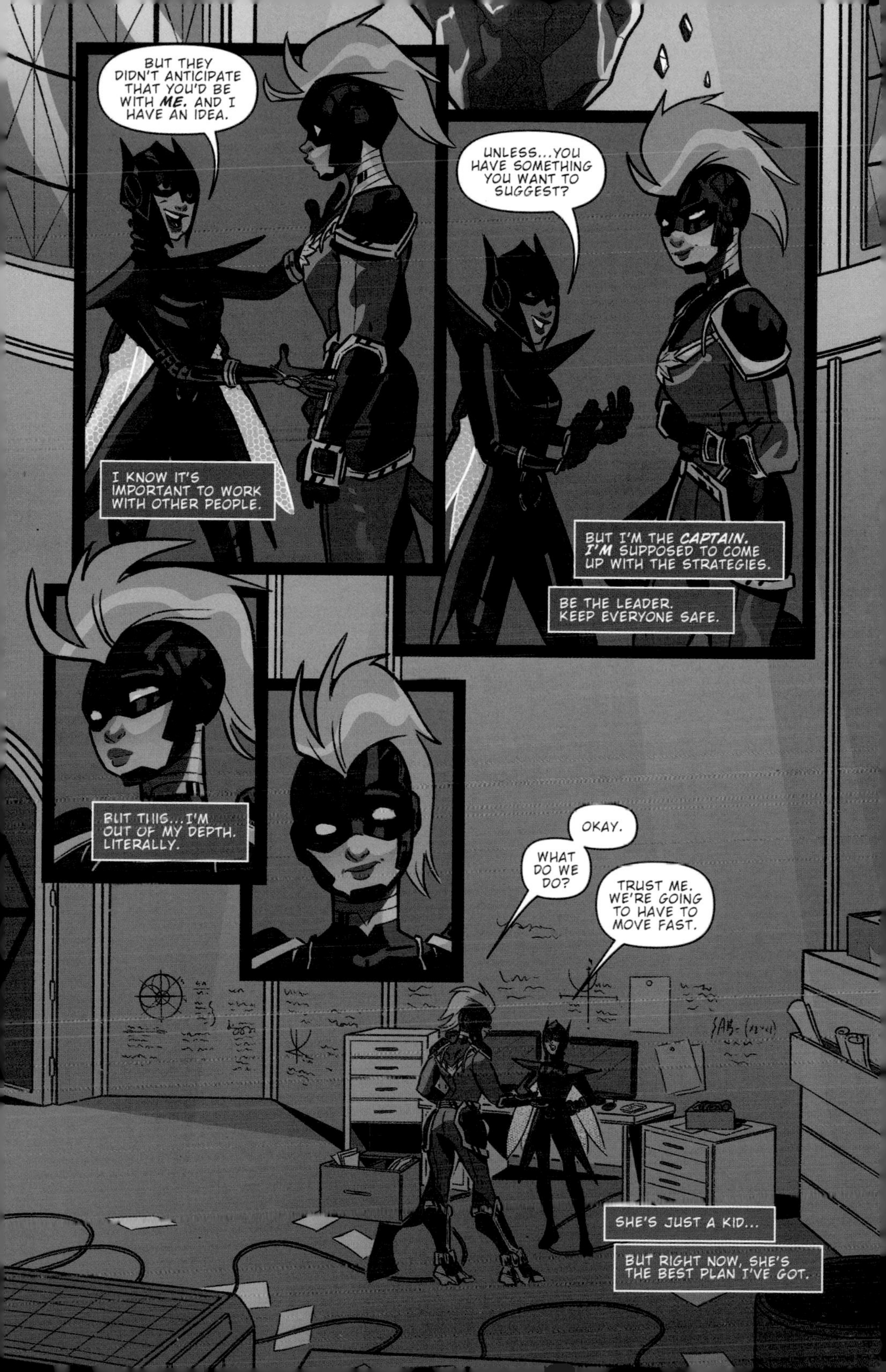
BUT THEY DIDN'T ANTICIPATE THAT YOU'D BE WITH ME. AND I HAVE AN IDEA.
I KNOW IT'S IMPORTANT TO WORK WITH OTHER PEOPLE.
UNLESS...YOU HAVE SOMETHING YOU WANT TO SUGGEST?
BUT I'M THE CAPTAIN. I'M SUPPOSED TO COME UP WITH THE STRATEGIES.
BE THE LEADER. KEEP EVERYONE SAFE.
BUT THIS...I'M OUT OF MY DEPTH. LITERALLY.
OKAY.
WHAT DO WE DO?
TRUST ME. WE'RE GOING TO HAVE TO MOVE FAST.
SHE'S JUST A KID...
BUT RIGHT NOW, SHE'S THE BEST PLAN I'VE GOT.

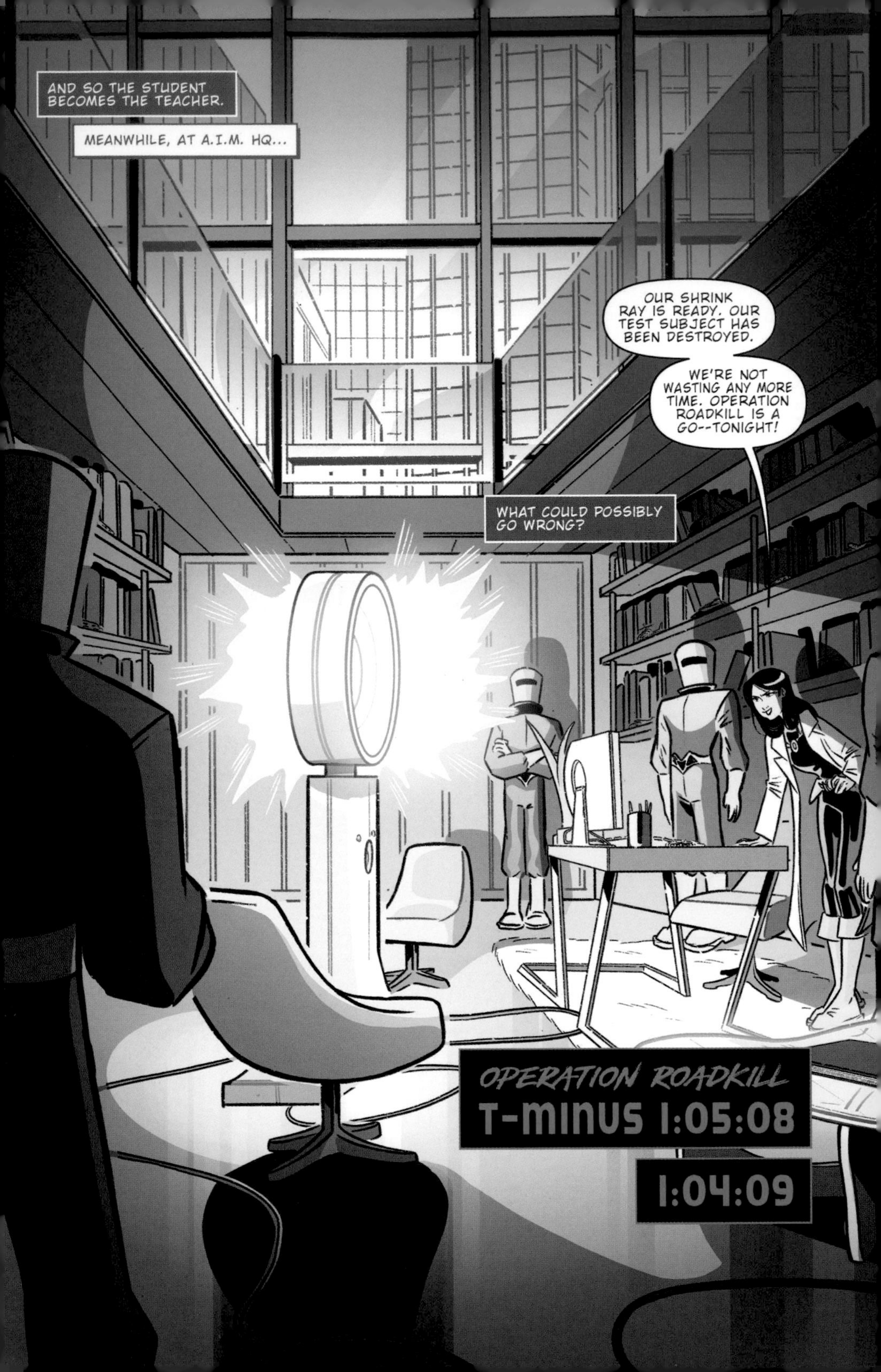
AND SO THE STUDENT BECOMES THE TEACHER.
MEANWHILE, AT A.I.M. HQ...
OUR SHRINK RAY IS READY. OUR TEST SUBJECT HAS BEEN DESTROYED.
WE'RE NOT WASTING ANY MORE TIME. OPERATION ROADKILL IS A GO--TONIGHT!
WHAT COULD POSSIBLY GO WRONG?
OPERATION ROADKILL
T-MINUS 1:05:08
1:04:09

ART BY: SWEENEY BOO

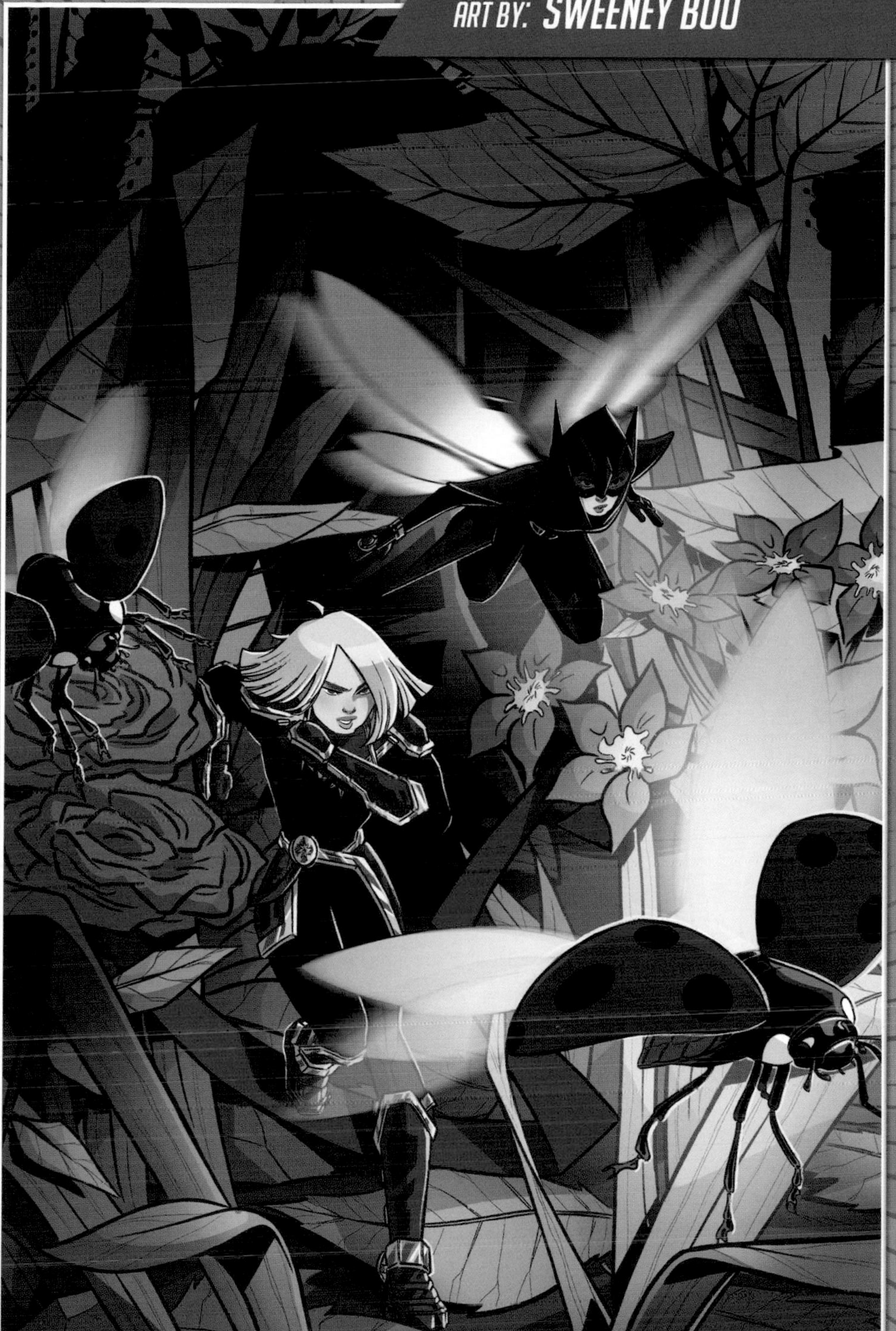

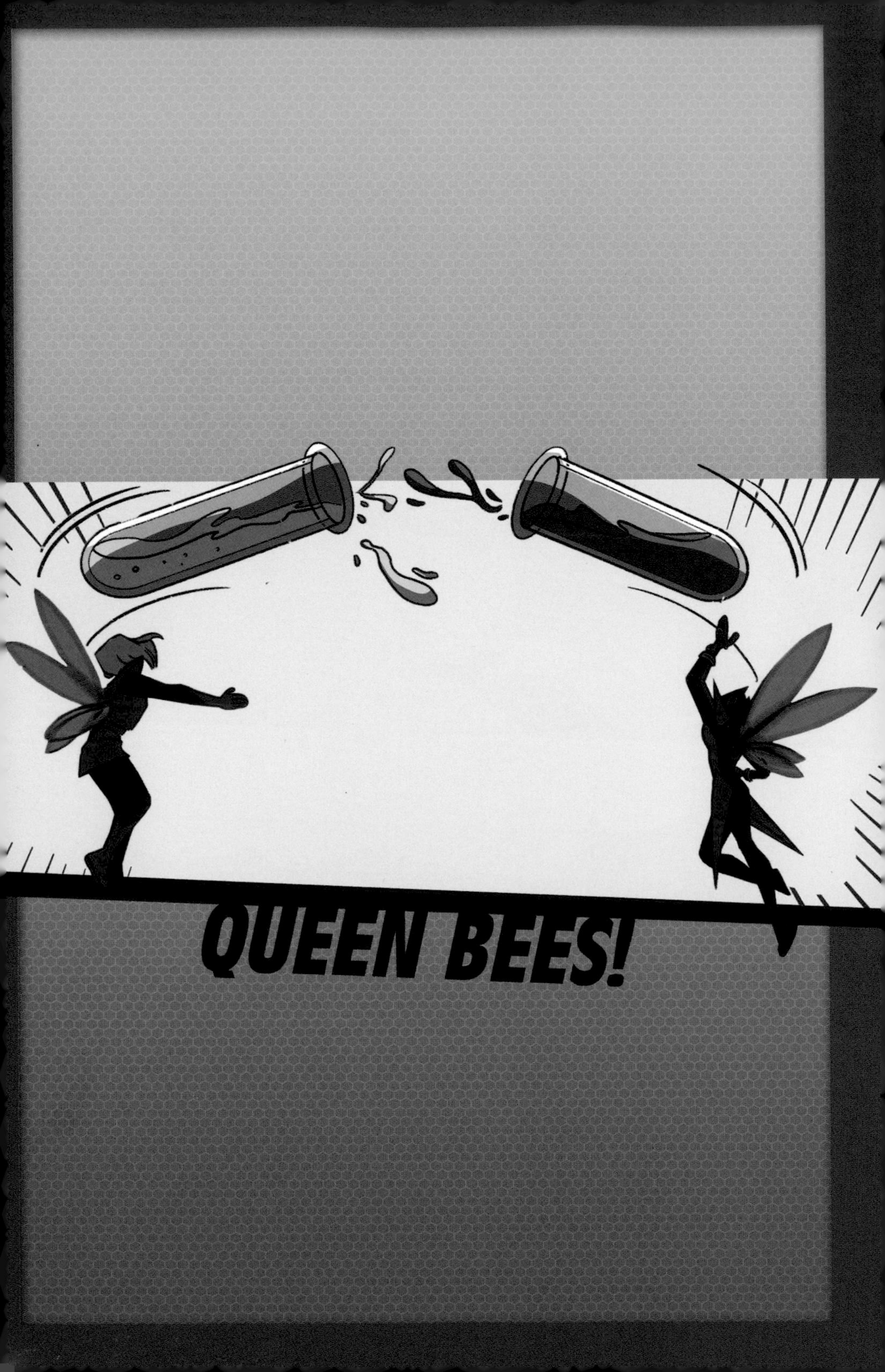
QUEEN BEES!

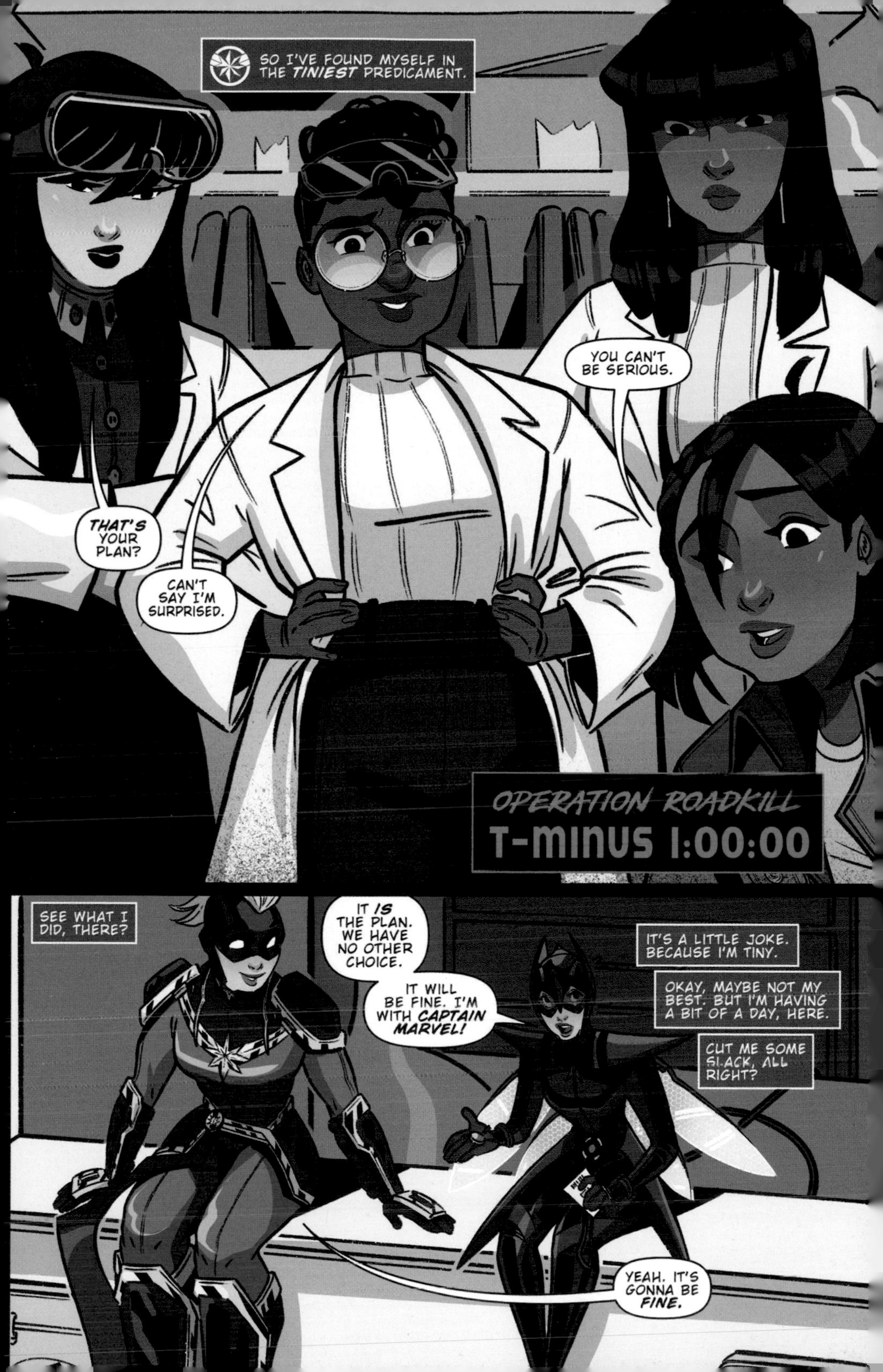
SO I'VE FOUND MYSELF IN THE *TINIEST* PREDICAMENT.
THAT'S YOUR PLAN?
CAN'T SAY I'M SURPRISED.
YOU CAN'T BE SERIOUS.
OPERATION ROADKILL
T-MINUS 1:00:00
SEE WHAT I DID, THERE?
IT *IS* THE PLAN. WE HAVE NO OTHER CHOICE.
IT WILL BE FINE. I'M WITH *CAPTAIN MARVEL!*
IT'S A LITTLE JOKE. BECAUSE I'M TINY.
OKAY, MAYBE NOT MY BEST. BUT I'M HAVING A BIT OF A DAY, HERE.
CUT ME SOME SLACK, ALL RIGHT?
YEAH. IT'S GONNA BE *FINE.*

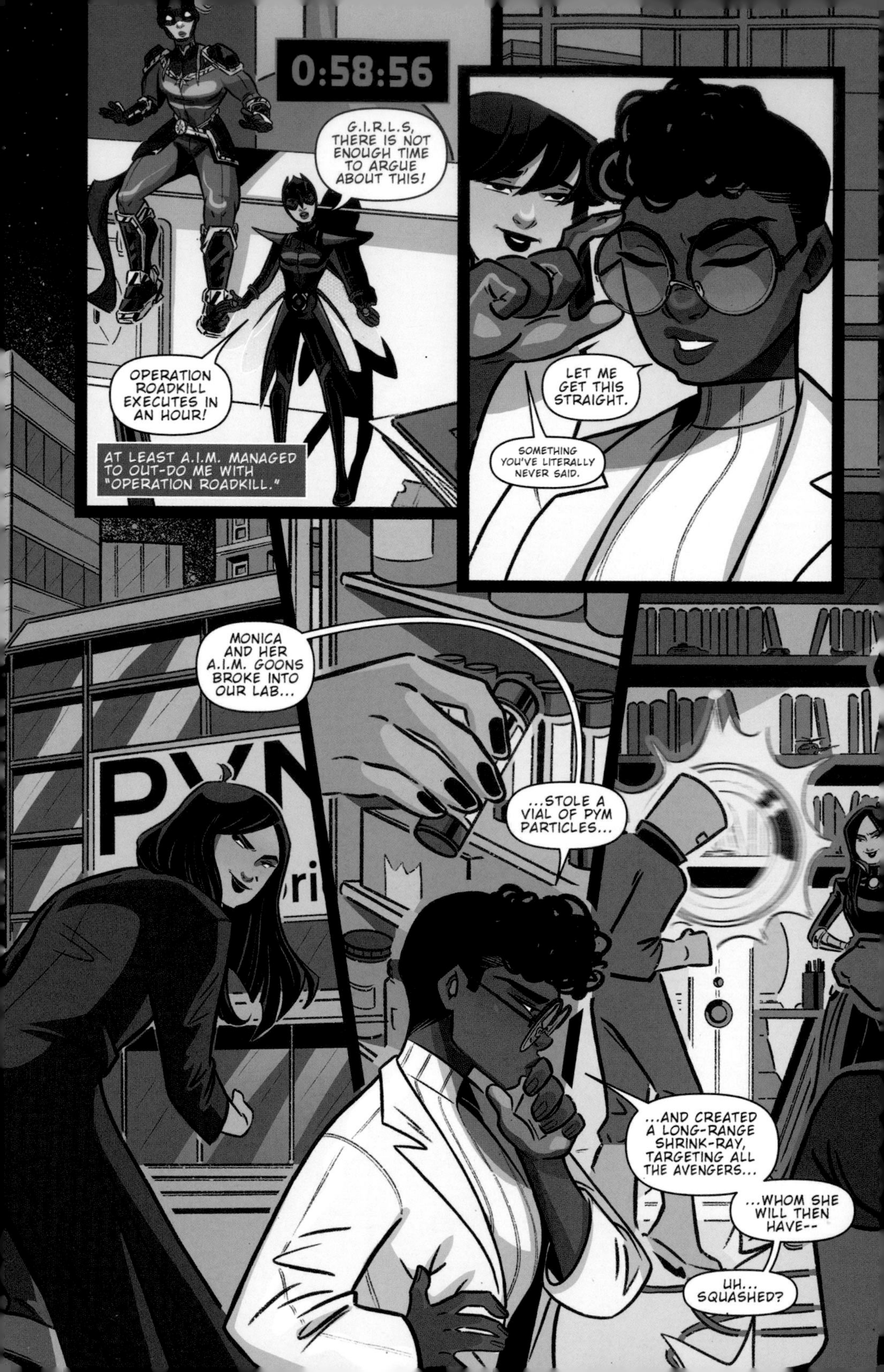
0:58:56
G.I.R.L.S, THERE IS NOT ENOUGH TIME TO ARGUE ABOUT THIS!
OPERATION ROADKILL EXECUTES IN AN HOUR!
AT LEAST A.I.M. MANAGED TO OUT-DO ME WITH "OPERATION ROADKILL."
LET ME GET THIS STRAIGHT.
SOMETHING YOU'VE LITERALLY NEVER SAID.
MONICA AND HER A.I.M. GOONS BROKE INTO OUR LAB...
...STOLE A VIAL OF PYM PARTICLES...
...AND CREATED A LONG-RANGE SHRINK-RAY, TARGETING ALL THE AVENGERS...
...WHOM SHE WILL THEN HAVE--
UH... SQUASHED?

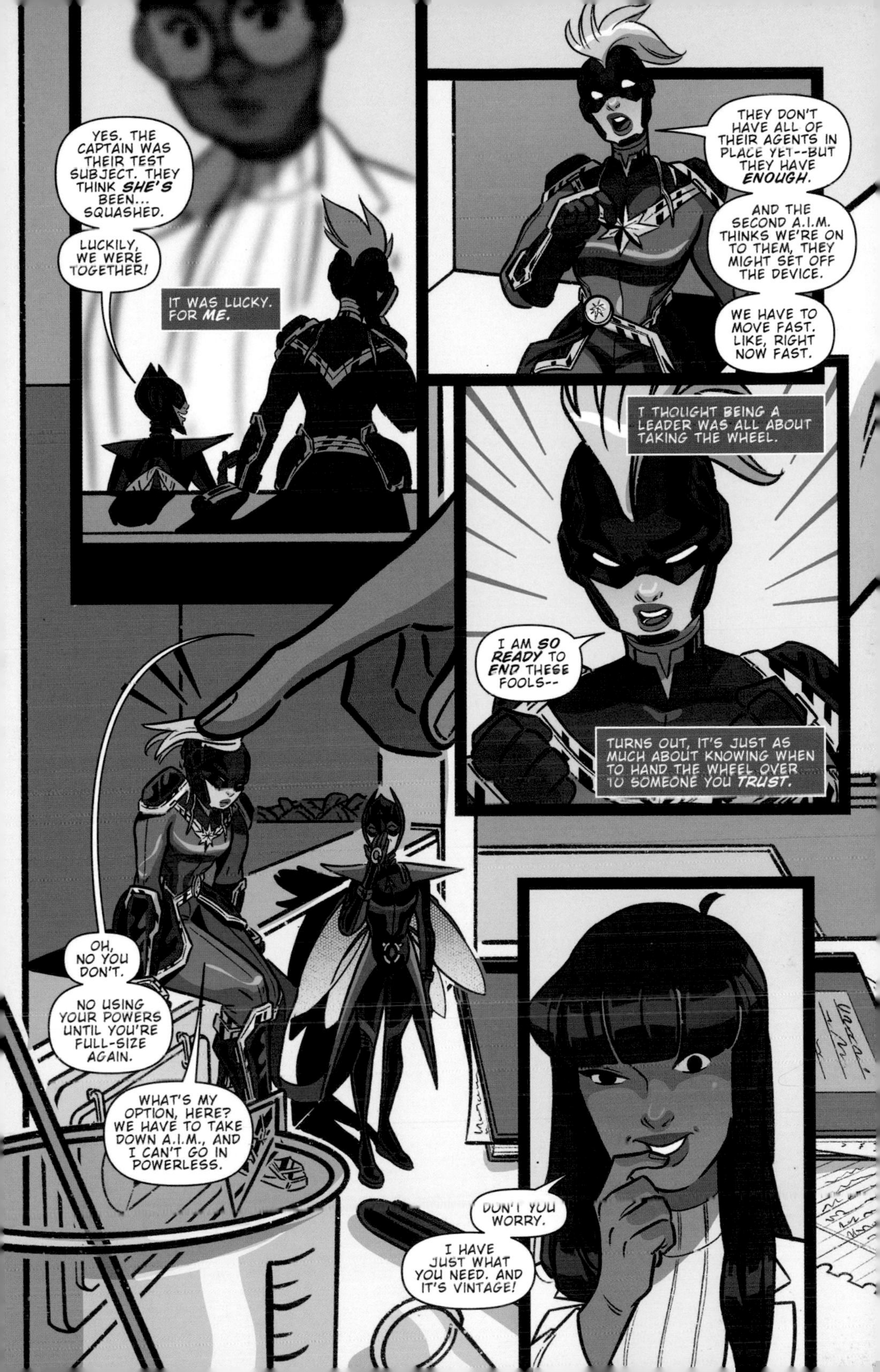
YES. THE CAPTAIN WAS THEIR TEST SUBJECT. THEY THINK SHE'S BEEN... SQUASHED.
LUCKILY, WE WERE TOGETHER!
IT WAS LUCKY. FOR ME.
THEY DON'T HAVE ALL OF THEIR AGENTS IN PLACE YET--BUT THEY HAVE ENOUGH.
AND THE SECOND A.I.M. THINKS WE'RE ON TO THEM, THEY MIGHT SET OFF THE DEVICE.
WE HAVE TO MOVE FAST. LIKE, RIGHT NOW FAST.
I THOUGHT BEING A LEADER WAS ALL ABOUT TAKING THE WHEEL.
I AM SO READY TO END THESE FOOLS--
TURNS OUT, IT'S JUST AS MUCH ABOUT KNOWING WHEN TO HAND THE WHEEL OVER TO SOMEONE YOU TRUST.
OH, NO YOU DON'T.
NO USING YOUR POWERS UNTIL YOU'RE FULL-SIZE AGAIN.
WHAT'S MY OPTION, HERE? WE HAVE TO TAKE DOWN A.I.M., AND I CAN'T GO IN POWERLESS.
DON'T YOU WORRY.
I HAVE JUST WHAT YOU NEED. AND IT'S VINTAGE!

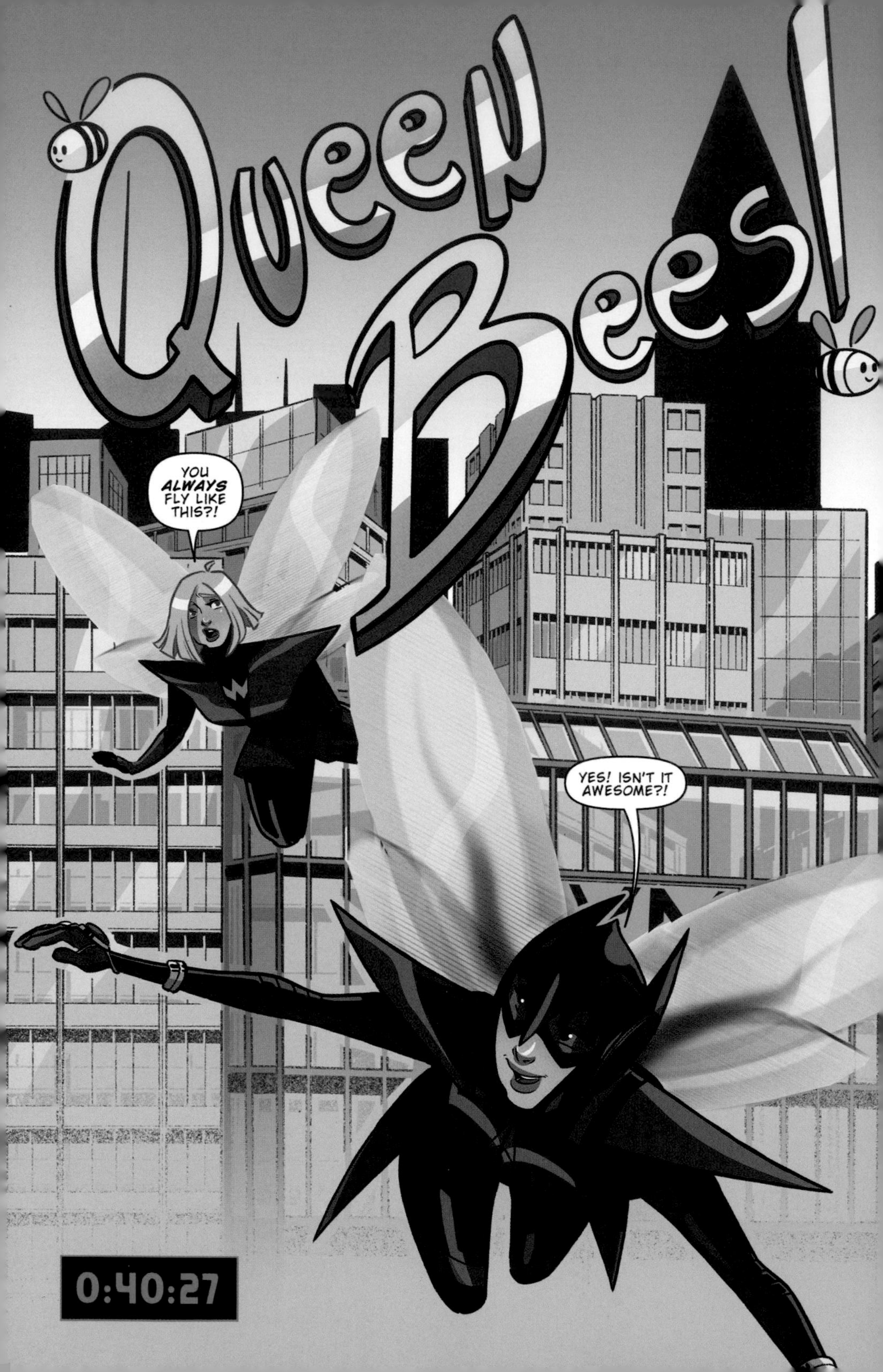
QUEEN BEES!
YOU ALWAYS FLY LIKE THIS?!
YES! ISN'T IT AWESOME?!
0:40:27

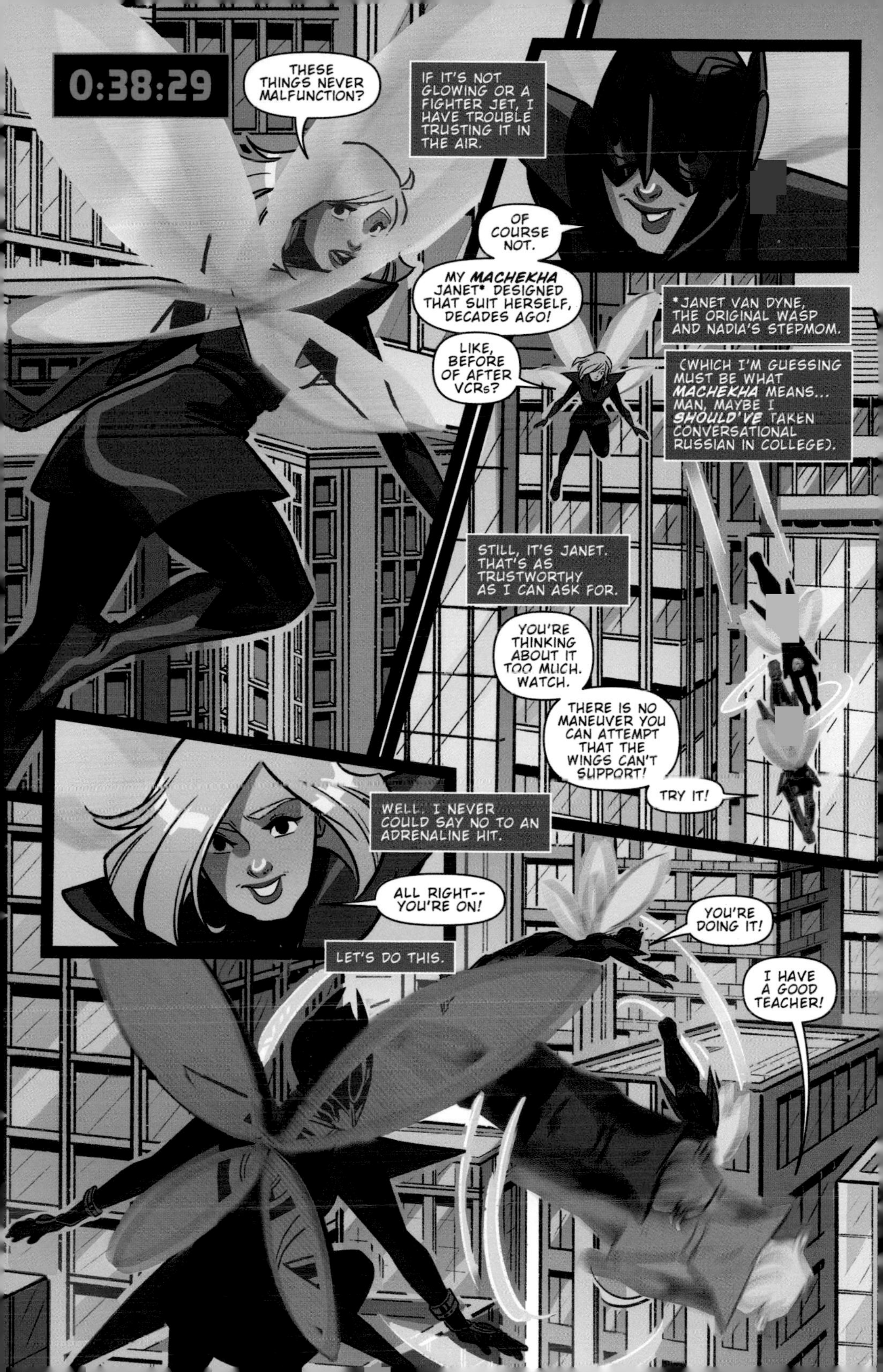
0:38:29
THESE THINGS NEVER MALFUNCTION?
IF IT'S NOT GLOWING OR A FIGHTER JET, I HAVE TROUBLE TRUSTING IT IN THE AIR.
OF COURSE NOT.
MY MACHEKHA JANET* DESIGNED THAT SUIT HERSELF, DECADES AGO!
*JANET VAN DYNE, THE ORIGINAL WASP AND NADIA'S STEPMOM.
LIKE, BEFORE OF AFTER VCRs?
(WHICH I'M GUESSING MUST BE WHAT MACHEKHA MEANS... MAN, MAYBE I SHOULD'VE TAKEN CONVERSATIONAL RUSSIAN IN COLLEGE).
STILL, IT'S JANET. THAT'S AS TRUSTWORTHY AS I CAN ASK FOR.
YOU'RE THINKING ABOUT IT TOO MUCH. WATCH.
THERE IS NO MANEUVER YOU CAN ATTEMPT THAT THE WINGS CAN'T SUPPORT!
TRY IT!
WELL. I NEVER COULD SAY NO TO AN ADRENALINE HIT.
ALL RIGHT-- YOU'RE ON!
LET'S DO THIS.
YOU'RE DOING IT!
I HAVE A GOOD TEACHER!

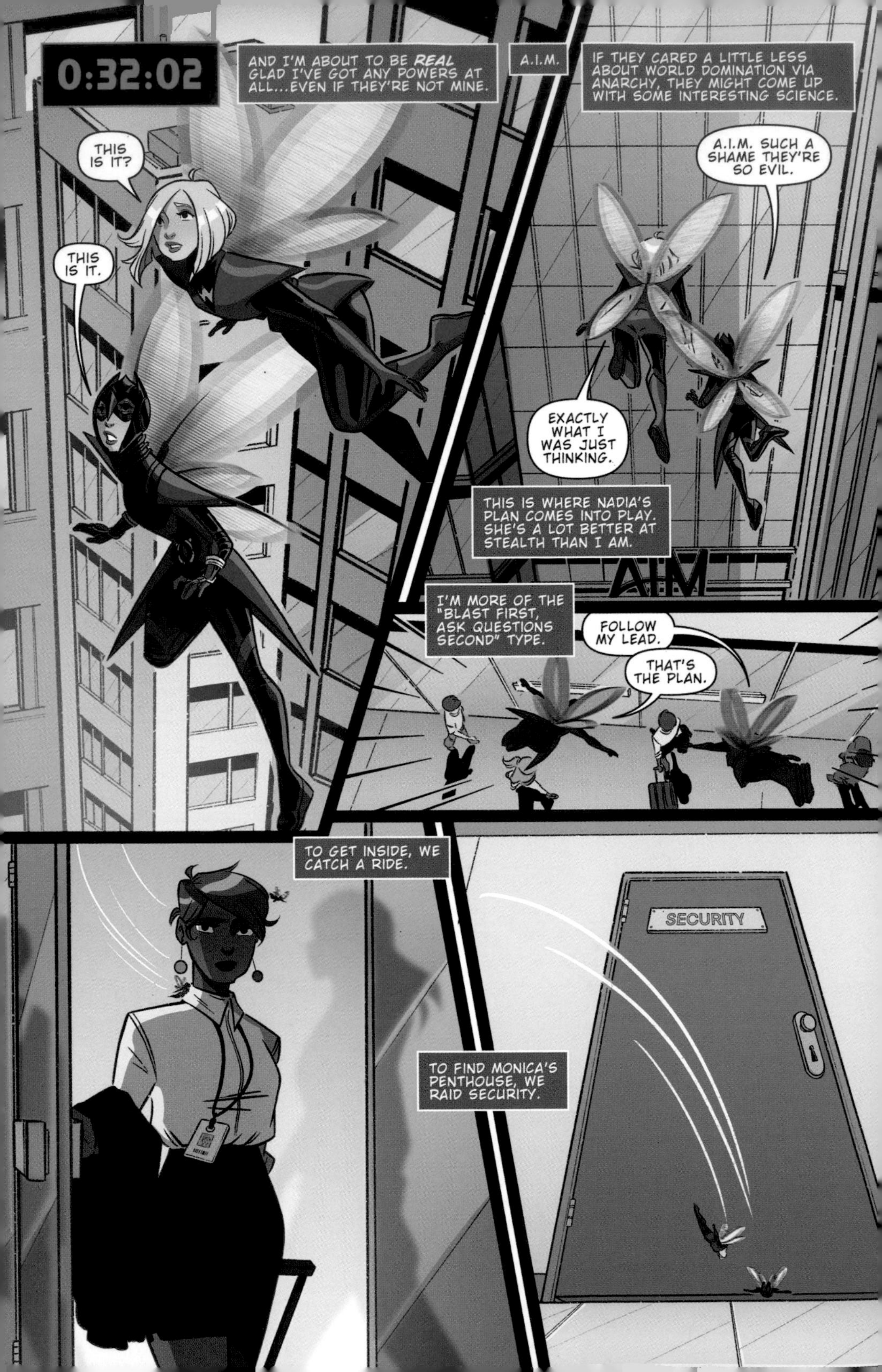
0:32:02
AND I'M ABOUT TO BE *REAL* GLAD I'VE GOT ANY POWERS AT ALL...EVEN IF THEY'RE NOT MINE.
THIS IS IT?
THIS IS IT.
A.I.M.
IF THEY CARED A LITTLE LESS ABOUT WORLD DOMINATION VIA ANARCHY, THEY MIGHT COME UP WITH SOME INTERESTING SCIENCE.
A.I.M. SUCH A SHAME THEY'RE SO EVIL.
EXACTLY WHAT I WAS JUST THINKING.
THIS IS WHERE NADIA'S PLAN COMES INTO PLAY. SHE'S A LOT BETTER AT STEALTH THAN I AM.
AIM
I'M MORE OF THE "BLAST FIRST, ASK QUESTIONS SECOND" TYPE.
FOLLOW MY LEAD.
THAT'S THE PLAN.
TO GET INSIDE, WE CATCH A RIDE.
TO FIND MONICA'S PENTHOUSE, WE RAID SECURITY.
SECURITY

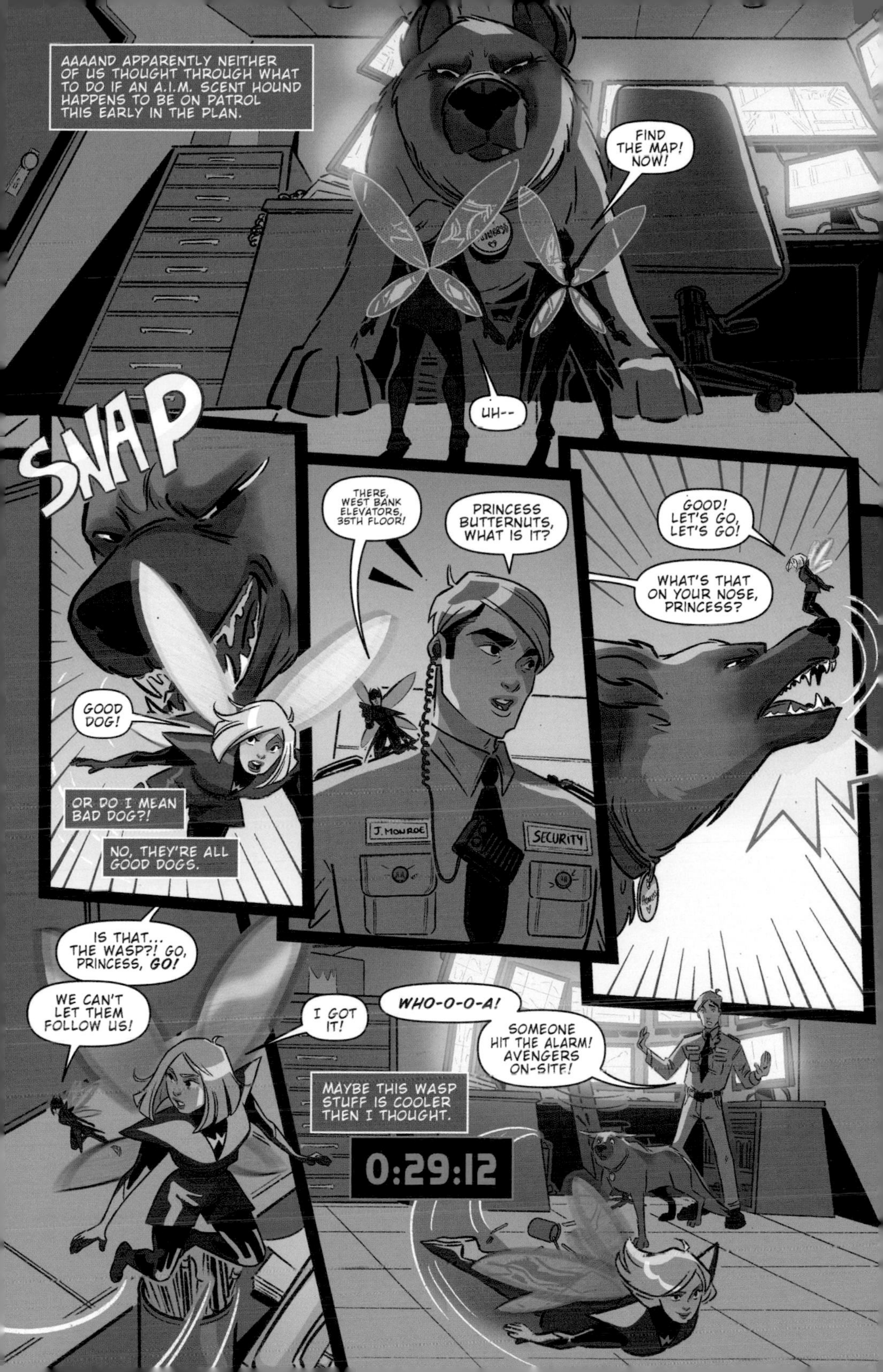
AAAAND APPARENTLY NEITHER OF US THOUGHT THROUGH WHAT TO DO IF AN A.I.M. SCENT HOUND HAPPENS TO BE ON PATROL THIS EARLY IN THE PLAN.
FIND THE MAP! NOW!
UH--
SNAP
GOOD DOG!
OR DO I MEAN BAD DOG?!
NO, THEY'RE ALL GOOD DOGS.
THERE, WEST BANK ELEVATORS, 35TH FLOOR!
PRINCESS BUTTERNUTS, WHAT IS IT?
J. MONROE
SECURITY
GOOD! LET'S GO, LET'S GO!
WHAT'S THAT ON YOUR NOSE, PRINCESS?
IS THAT... THE WASP?! GO, PRINCESS, GO!
WE CAN'T LET THEM FOLLOW US!
I GOT IT!
WHO-O-O-A!
SOMEONE HIT THE ALARM! AVENGERS ON-SITE!
MAYBE THIS WASP STUFF IS COOLER THEN I THOUGHT.
0:29:12

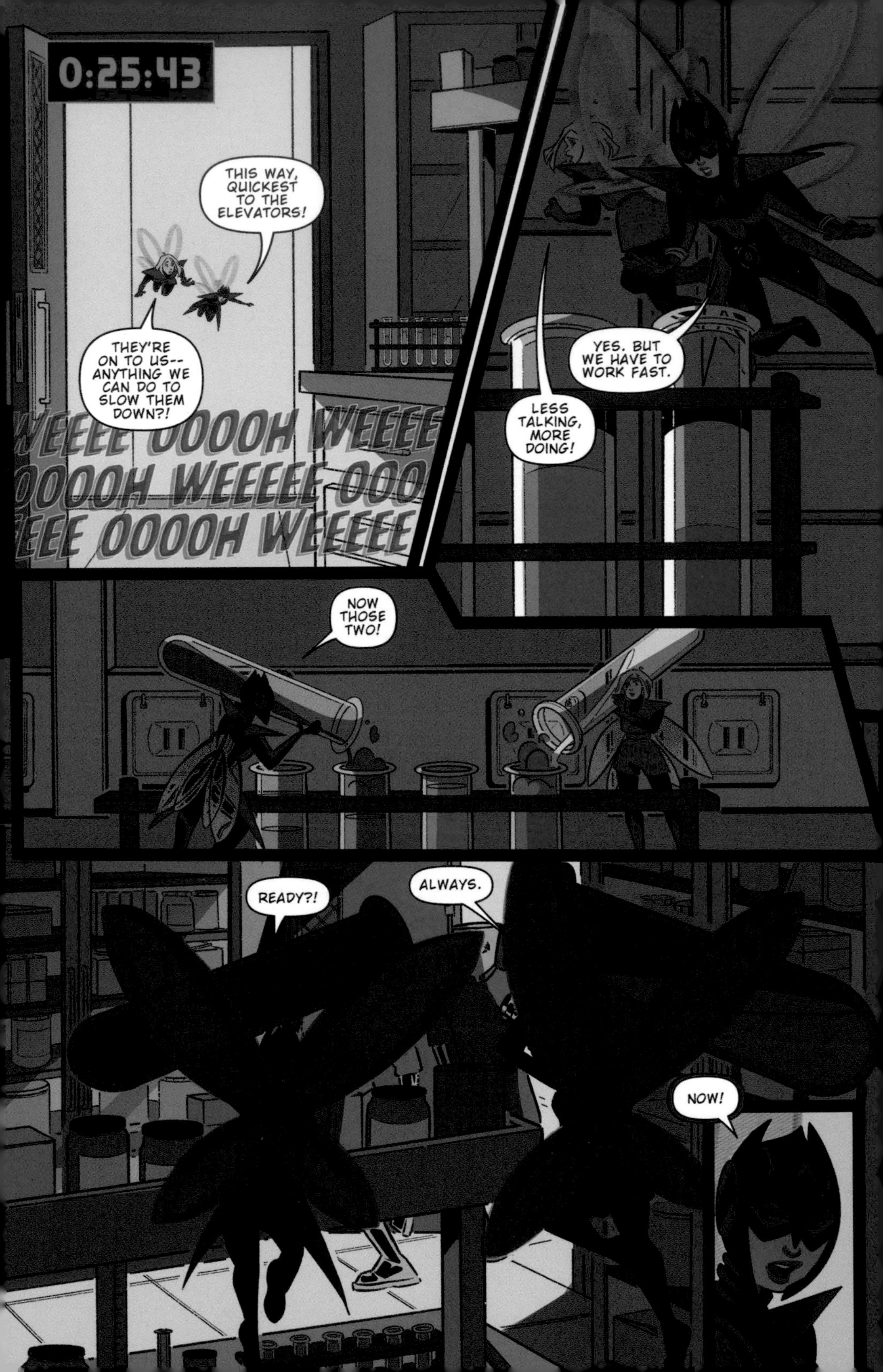
0:25:43
THIS WAY, QUICKEST TO THE ELEVATORS!
THEY'RE ON TO US--ANYTHING WE CAN DO TO SLOW THEM DOWN?!
WEEEE OOOOH WEEEE OOOOH WEEEEE OOO EEE OOOOH WEEEEE
YES. BUT WE HAVE TO WORK FAST.
LESS TALKING, MORE DOING!
NOW THOSE TWO!
READY?!
ALWAYS.
NOW!

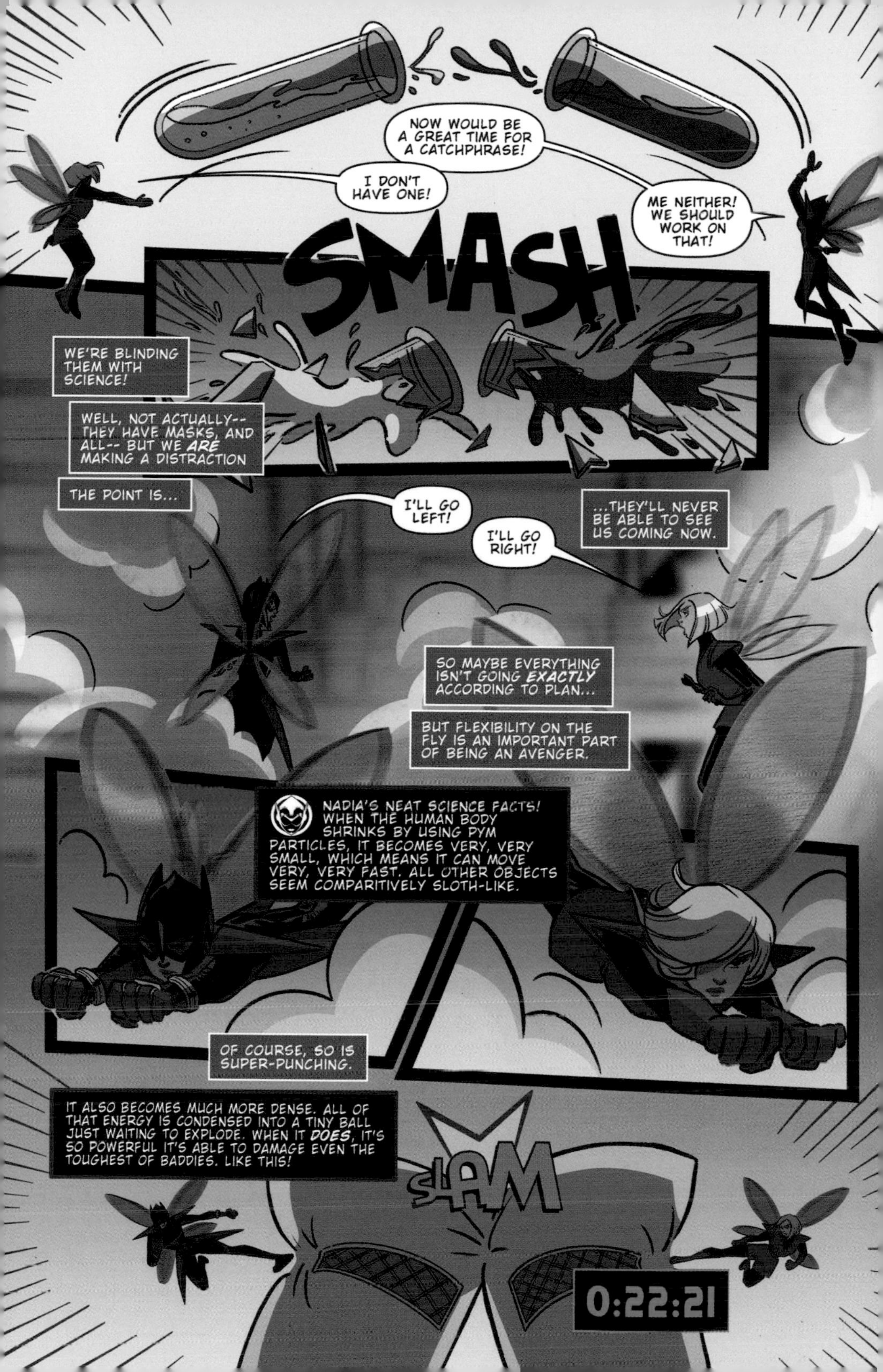
NOW WOULD BE A GREAT TIME FOR A CATCHPHRASE!
I DON'T HAVE ONE!
ME NEITHER! WE SHOULD WORK ON THAT!
SMASH
WE'RE BLINDING THEM WITH SCIENCE!
WELL, NOT ACTUALLY-- THEY HAVE MASKS, AND ALL-- BUT WE *ARE* MAKING A DISTRACTION
THE POINT IS...
I'LL GO LEFT!
I'LL GO RIGHT!
...THEY'LL NEVER BE ABLE TO SEE US COMING NOW.
SO MAYBE EVERYTHING ISN'T GOING *EXACTLY* ACCORDING TO PLAN...
BUT FLEXIBILITY ON THE FLY IS AN IMPORTANT PART OF BEING AN AVENGER.
NADIA'S NEAT SCIENCE FACTS! WHEN THE HUMAN BODY SHRINKS BY USING PYM PARTICLES, IT BECOMES VERY, VERY SMALL, WHICH MEANS IT CAN MOVE VERY, VERY FAST. ALL OTHER OBJECTS SEEM COMPARITIVELY SLOTH-LIKE.
OF COURSE, SO IS SUPER-PUNCHING.
IT ALSO BECOMES MUCH MORE DENSE. ALL OF THAT ENERGY IS CONDENSED INTO A TINY BALL JUST WAITING TO EXPLODE. WHEN IT *DOES*, IT'S SO POWERFUL IT'S ABLE TO DAMAGE EVEN THE TOUGHEST OF BADDIES. LIKE THIS!
SLAM
0:22:21

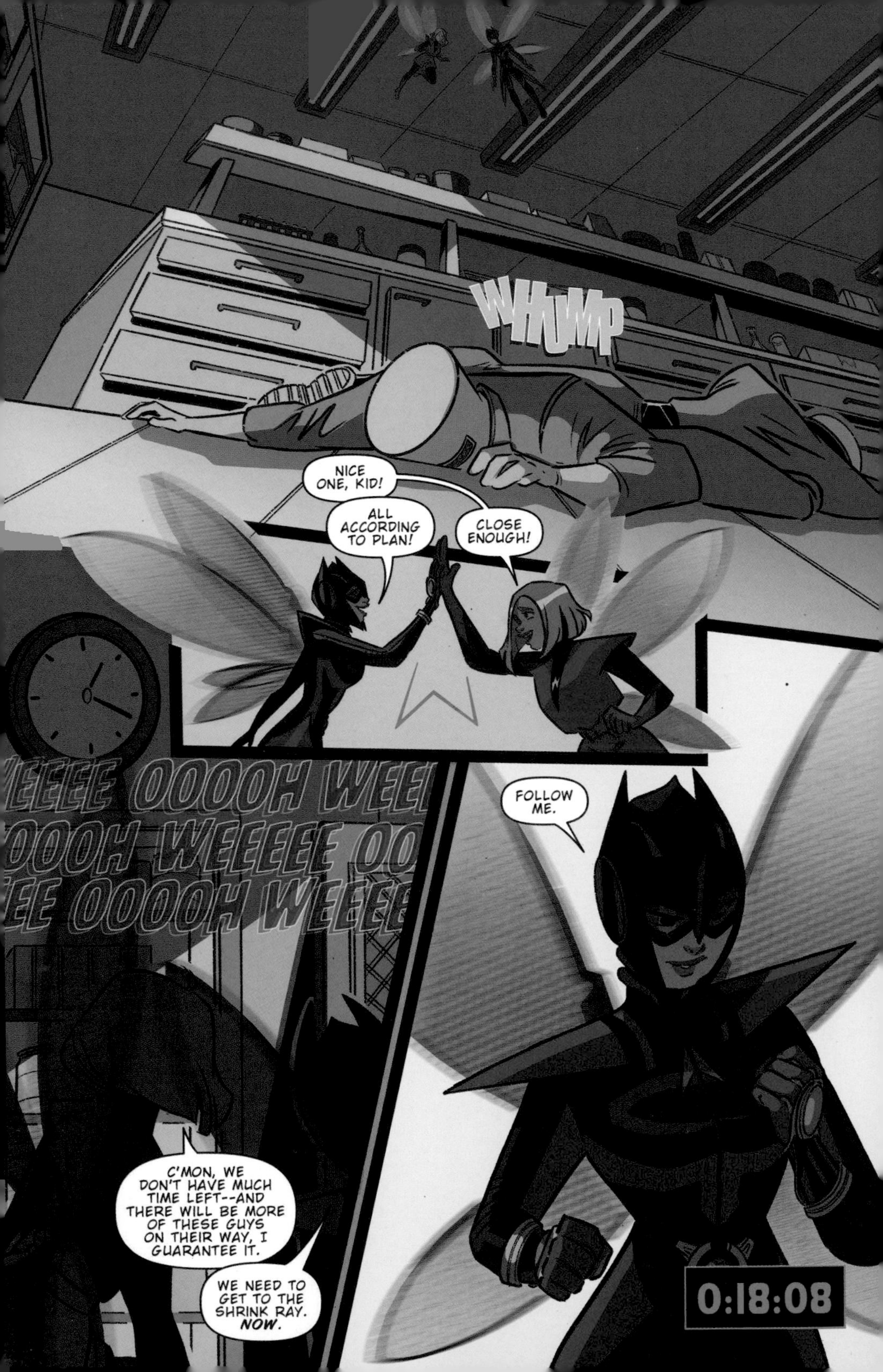
WHUMP
NICE ONE, KID!
ALL ACCORDING TO PLAN!
CLOSE ENOUGH!
WEEEE OOOOH WEEE
OOOOH WEEEEE OO
EE OOOOH WEEEE
FOLLOW ME.
C'MON, WE DON'T HAVE MUCH TIME LEFT--AND THERE WILL BE MORE OF THESE GUYS ON THEIR WAY, I GUARANTEE IT.
WE NEED TO GET TO THE SHRINK RAY. *NOW*.
0:18:08

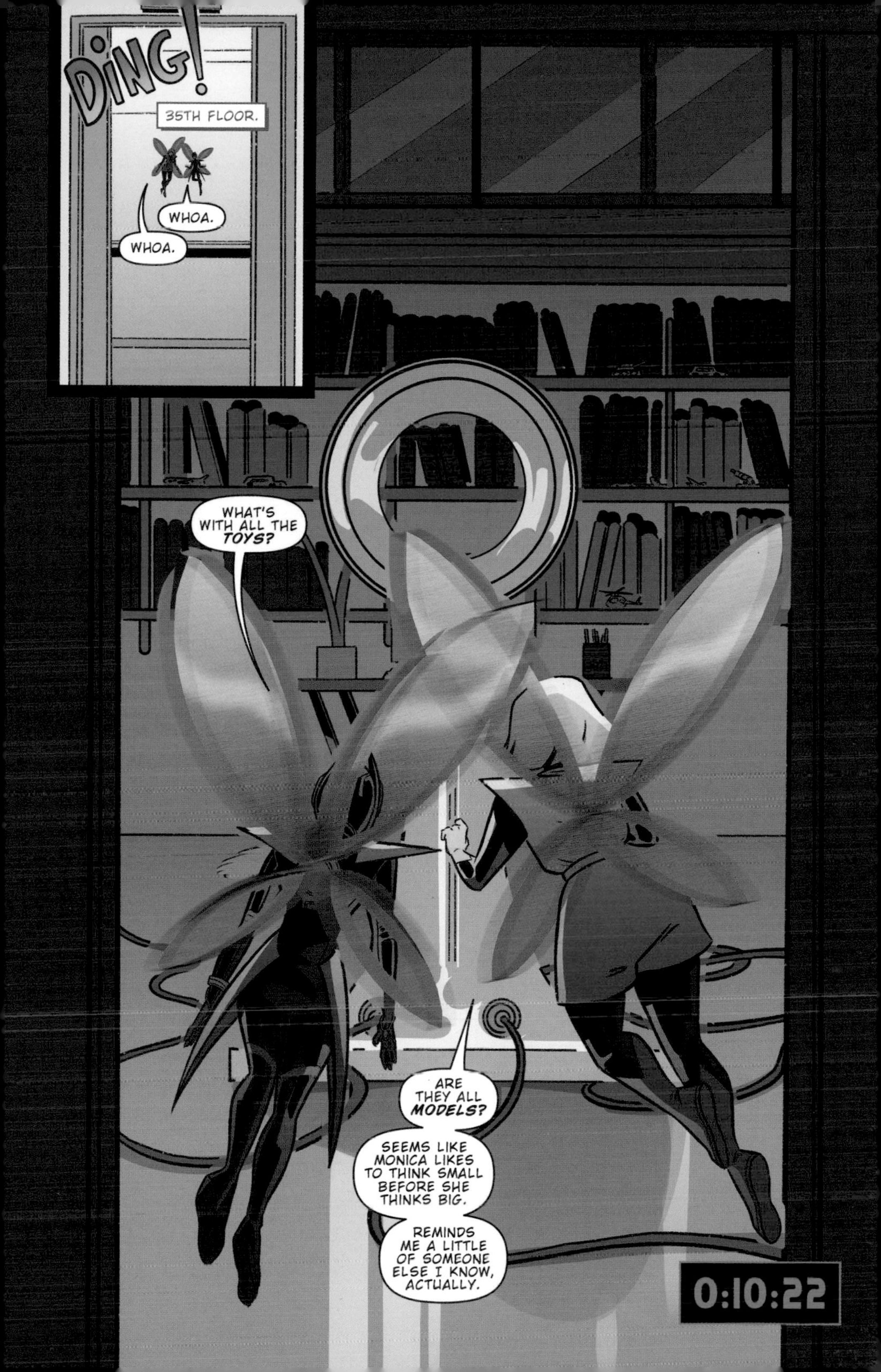
DING!
35TH FLOOR.
WHOA.
WHOA.
WHAT'S WITH ALL THE *TOYS?*
ARE THEY ALL *MODELS?*
SEEMS LIKE MONICA LIKES TO THINK SMALL BEFORE SHE THINKS BIG.
REMINDS ME A LITTLE OF SOMEONE ELSE I KNOW, ACTUALLY.
0:10:22

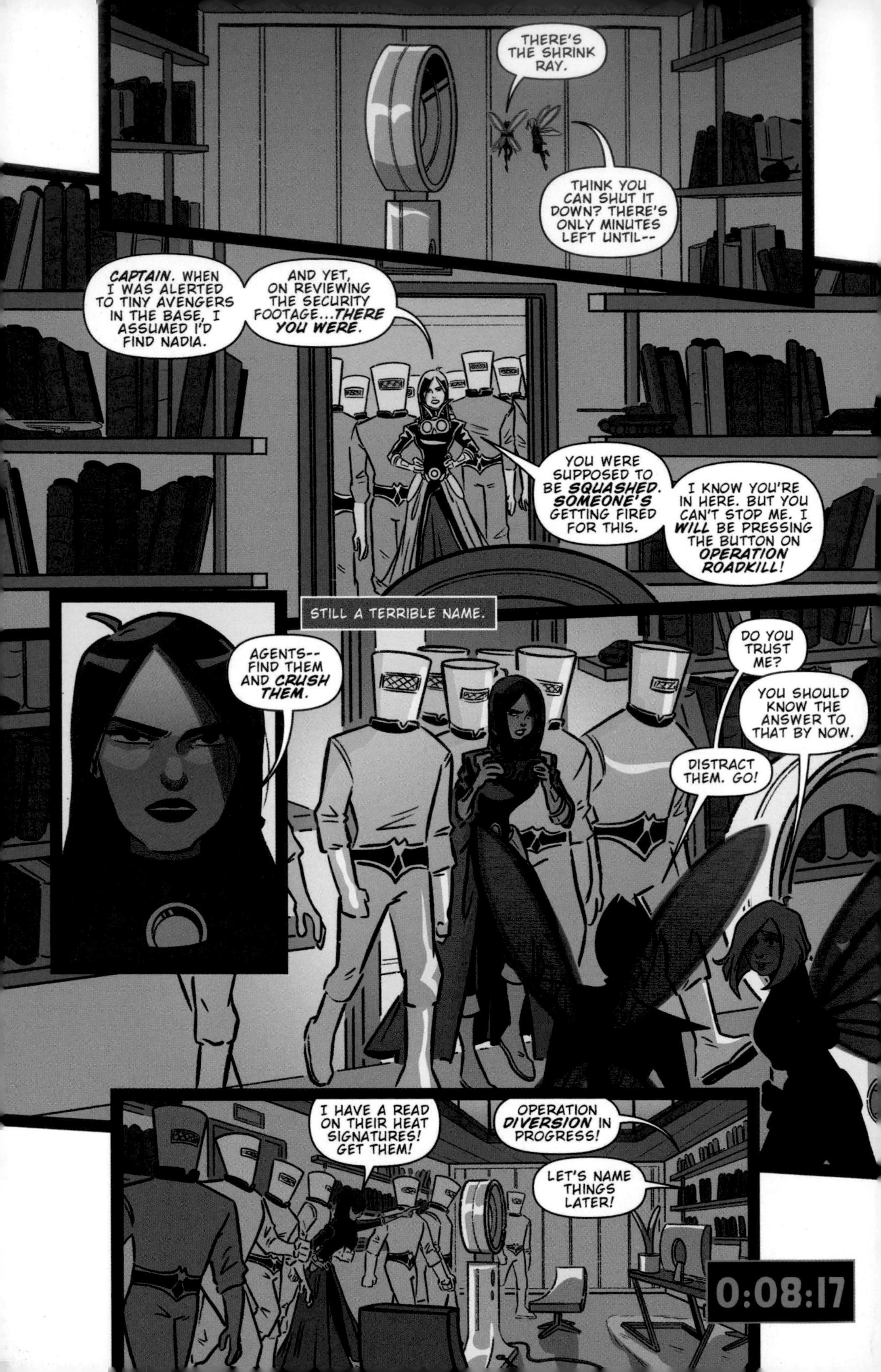
THERE'S THE SHRINK RAY.
THINK YOU CAN SHUT IT DOWN? THERE'S ONLY MINUTES LEFT UNTIL--
CAPTAIN. WHEN I WAS ALERTED TO TINY AVENGERS IN THE BASE, I ASSUMED I'D FIND NADIA.
AND YET, ON REVIEWING THE SECURITY FOOTAGE...THERE YOU WERE.
YOU WERE SUPPOSED TO BE SQUASHED. SOMEONE'S GETTING FIRED FOR THIS.
I KNOW YOU'RE IN HERE. BUT YOU CAN'T STOP ME. I WILL BE PRESSING THE BUTTON ON OPERATION ROADKILL!
STILL A TERRIBLE NAME.
AGENTS-- FIND THEM AND CRUSH THEM.
DO YOU TRUST ME?
YOU SHOULD KNOW THE ANSWER TO THAT BY NOW.
DISTRACT THEM. GO!
I HAVE A READ ON THEIR HEAT SIGNATURES! GET THEM!
OPERATION DIVERSION IN PROGRESS!
LET'S NAME THINGS LATER!
0:08:17

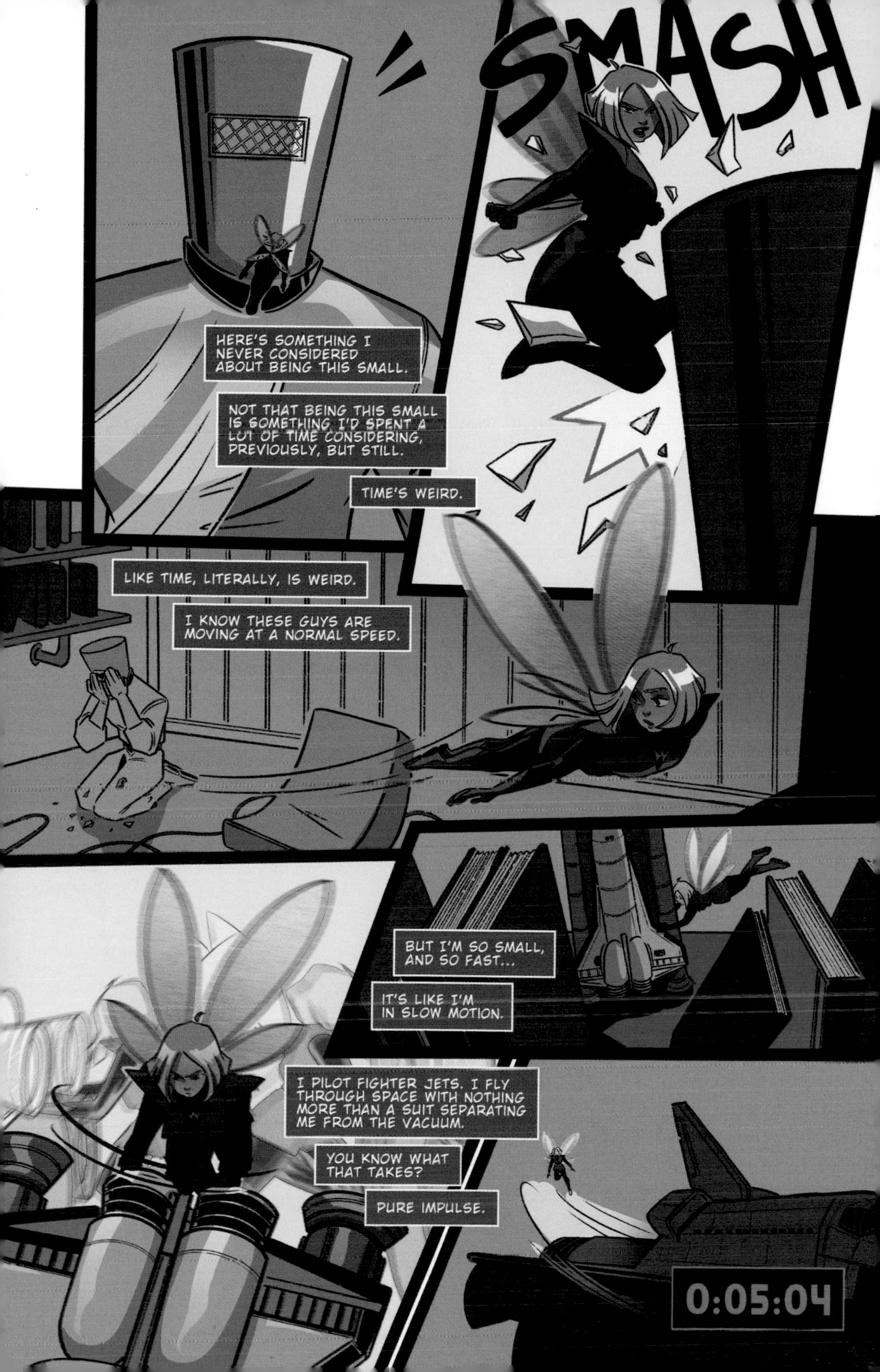
SMASH
HERE'S SOMETHING I NEVER CONSIDERED ABOUT BEING THIS SMALL.
NOT THAT BEING THIS SMALL IS SOMETHING I'D SPENT A LOT OF TIME CONSIDERING, PREVIOUSLY, BUT STILL.
TIME'S WEIRD.
LIKE TIME, LITERALLY, IS WEIRD.
I KNOW THESE GUYS ARE MOVING AT A NORMAL SPEED.
BUT I'M SO SMALL, AND SO FAST...
IT'S LIKE I'M IN SLOW MOTION.
I PILOT FIGHTER JETS. I FLY THROUGH SPACE WITH NOTHING MORE THAN A SUIT SEPARATING ME FROM THE VACUUM.
YOU KNOW WHAT THAT TAKES?
PURE IMPULSE.
0:05:04

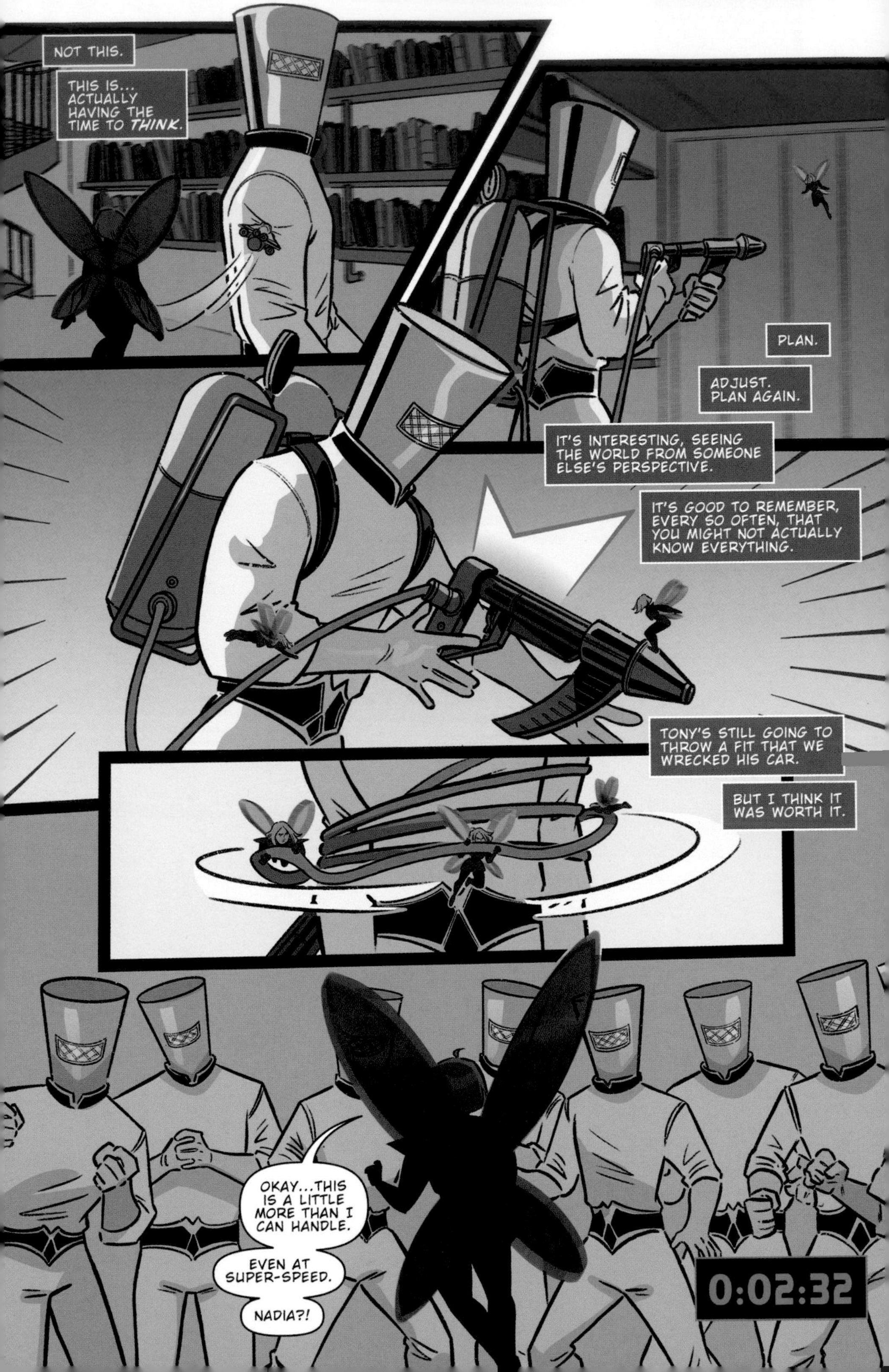
NOT THIS.
THIS IS... ACTUALLY HAVING THE TIME TO THINK.
PLAN.
ADJUST. PLAN AGAIN.
IT'S INTERESTING, SEEING THE WORLD FROM SOMEONE ELSE'S PERSPECTIVE.
IT'S GOOD TO REMEMBER, EVERY SO OFTEN, THAT YOU MIGHT NOT ACTUALLY KNOW EVERYTHING.
TONY'S STILL GOING TO THROW A FIT THAT WE WRECKED HIS CAR.
BUT I THINK IT WAS WORTH IT.
OKAY...THIS IS A LITTLE MORE THAN I CAN HANDLE.
EVEN AT SUPER-SPEED.
NADIA?!
0:02:32

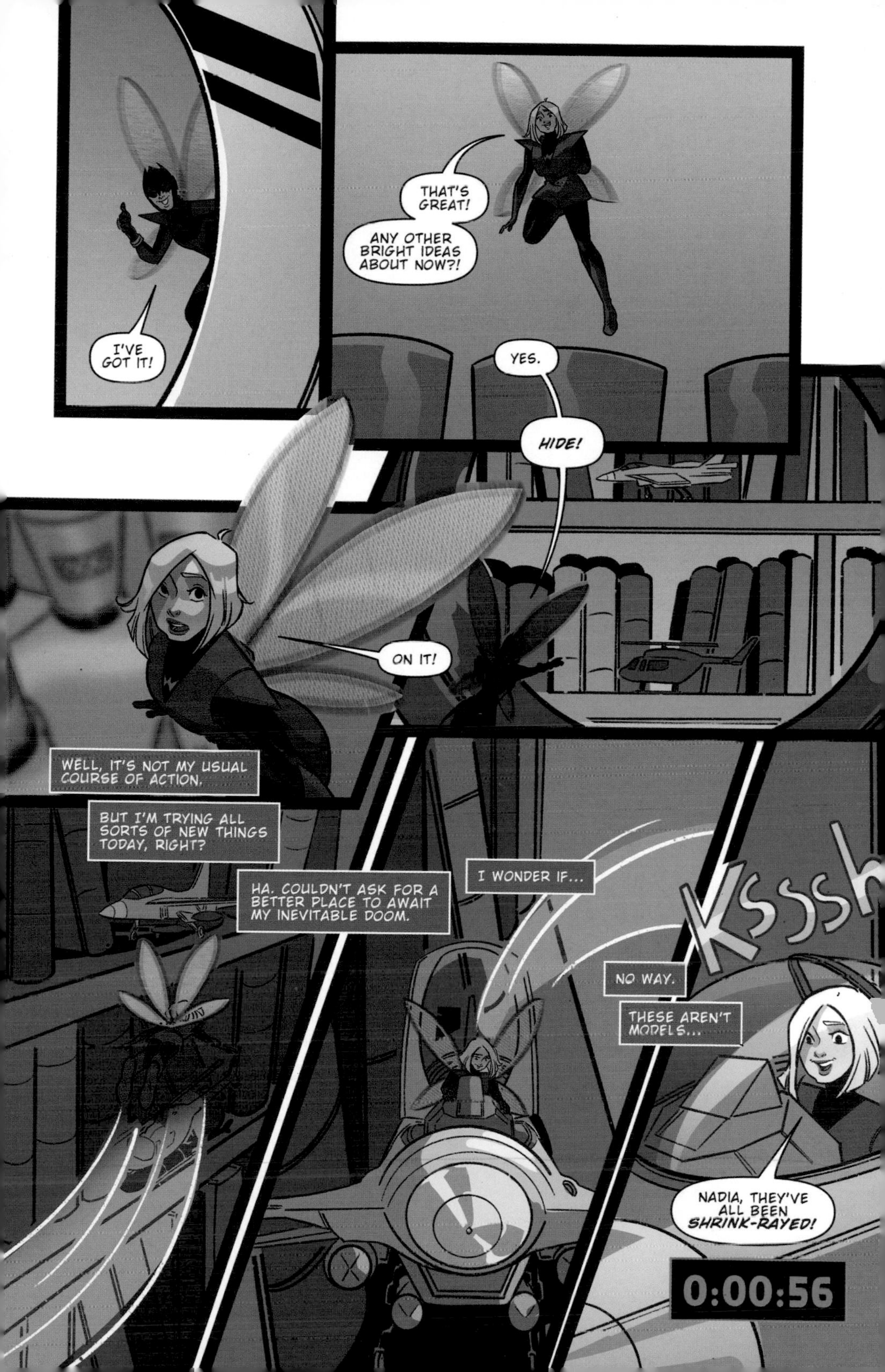
I'VE GOT IT!
THAT'S GREAT!
ANY OTHER BRIGHT IDEAS ABOUT NOW?!
YES.
HIDE!
ON IT!
WELL, IT'S NOT MY USUAL COURSE OF ACTION.
BUT I'M TRYING ALL SORTS OF NEW THINGS TODAY, RIGHT?
HA. COULDN'T ASK FOR A BETTER PLACE TO AWAIT MY INEVITABLE DOOM.
I WONDER IF...
Ksssh
NO WAY.
THESE AREN'T MODELS...
NADIA, THEY'VE ALL BEEN SHRINK-RAYED!
0:00:56

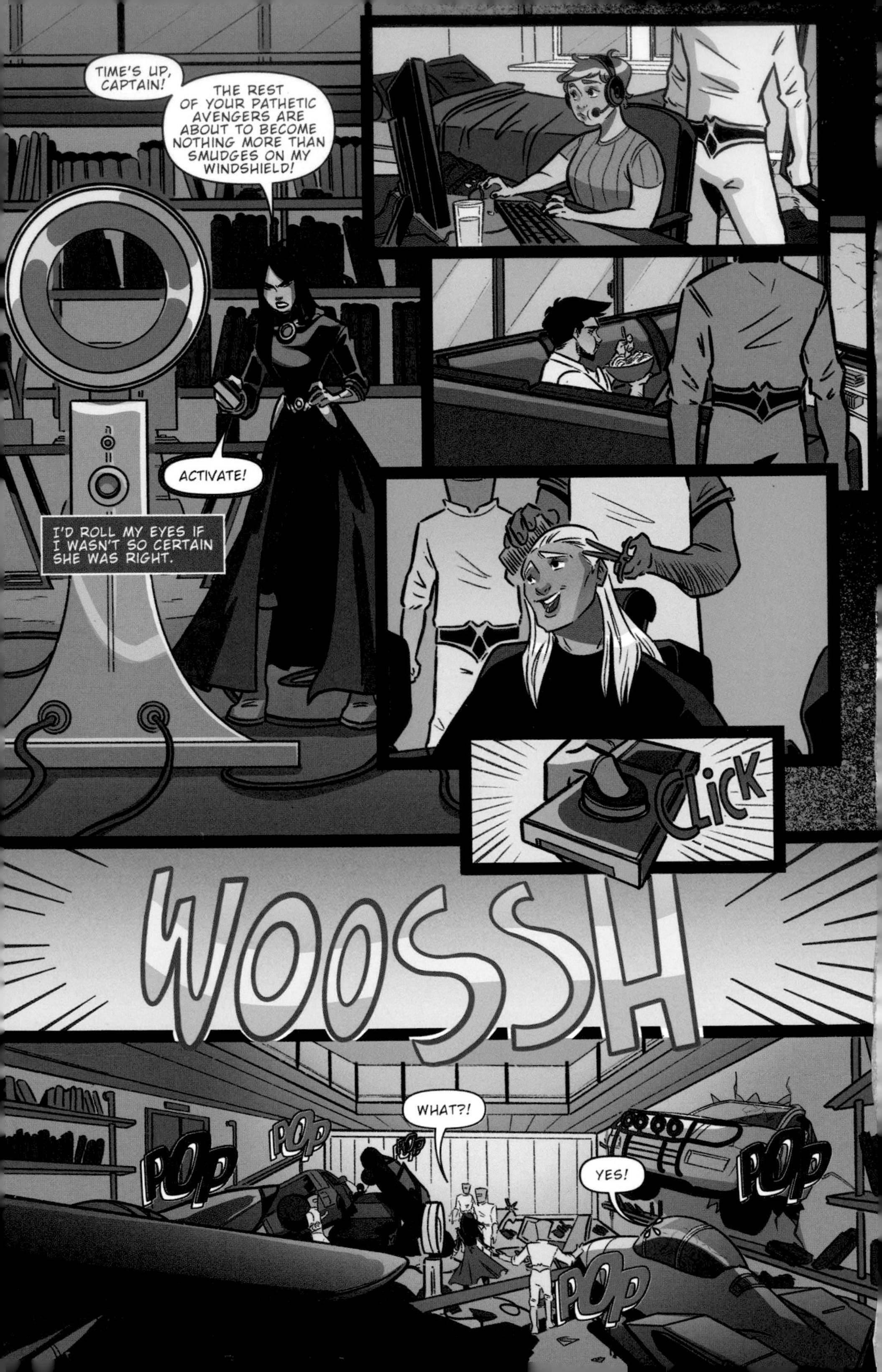
TIME'S UP, CAPTAIN!
THE REST OF YOUR PATHETIC AVENGERS ARE ABOUT TO BECOME NOTHING MORE THAN SMUDGES ON MY WINDSHIELD!
ACTIVATE!
I'D ROLL MY EYES IF I WASN'T SO CERTAIN SHE WAS RIGHT.
CLICK
WOOSSH
WHAT?!
YES!
POP
POP
POP
POP
POP

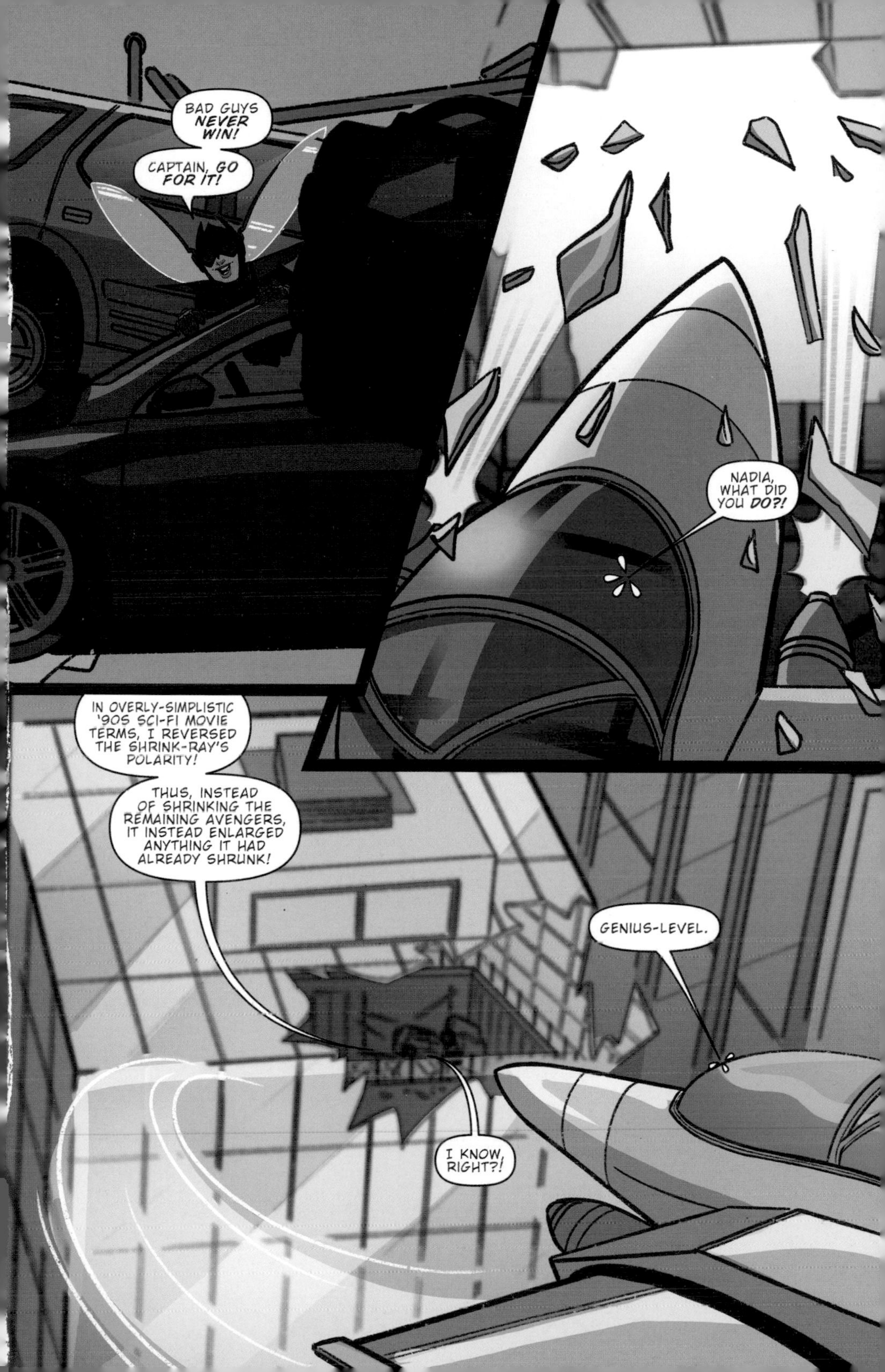
BAD GUYS NEVER WIN!
CAPTAIN, GO FOR IT!
NADIA, WHAT DID YOU DO?!
IN OVERLY-SIMPLISTIC '90S SCI-FI MOVIE TERMS, I REVERSED THE SHRINK-RAY'S POLARITY!
THUS, INSTEAD OF SHRINKING THE REMAINING AVENGERS, IT INSTEAD ENLARGED ANYTHING IT HAD ALREADY SHRUNK!
GENIUS-LEVEL.
I KNOW, RIGHT?!

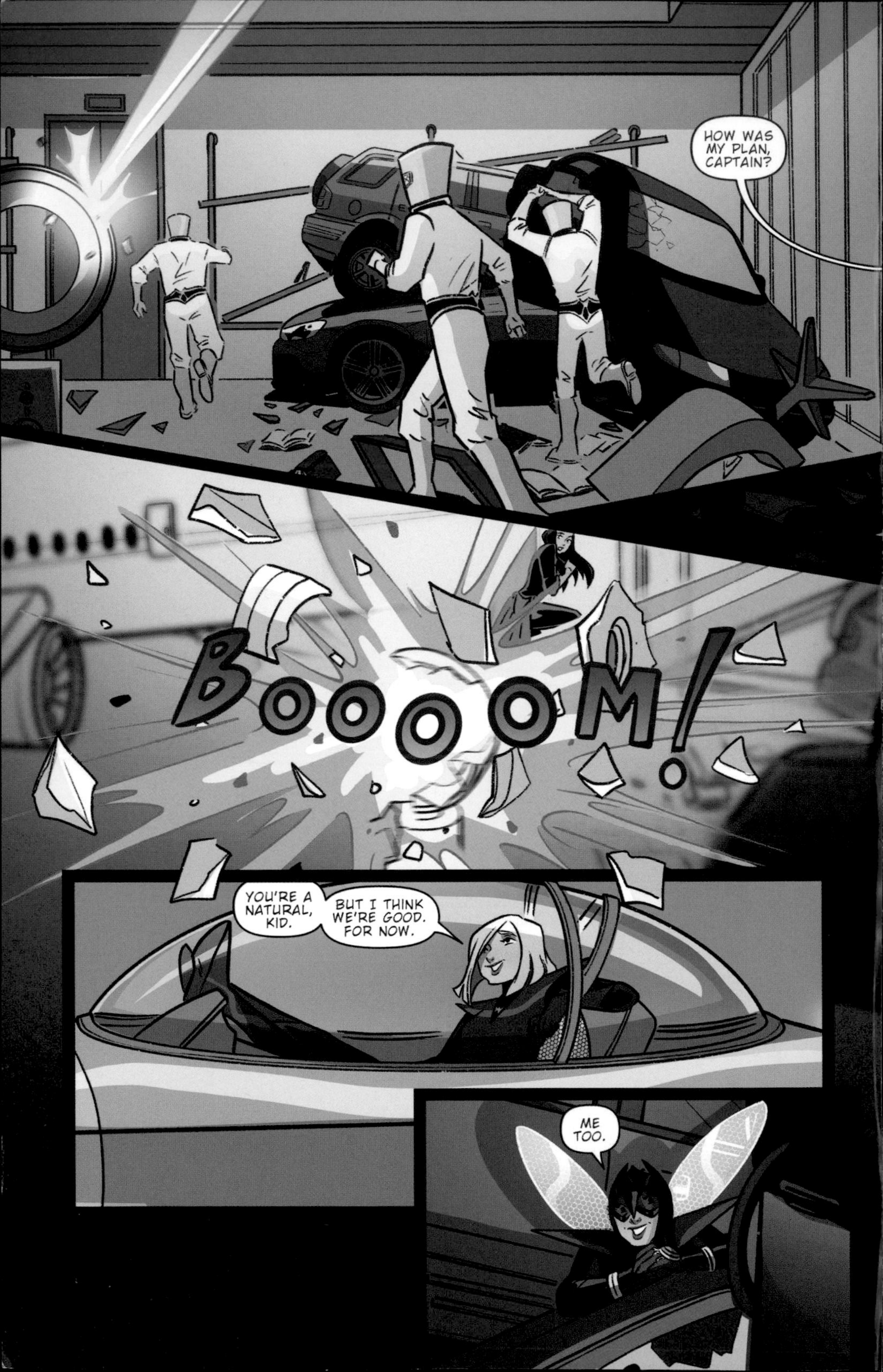
HOW WAS MY PLAN, CAPTAIN?
BOOOOM!
YOU'RE A NATURAL, KID.
BUT I THINK WE'RE GOOD. FOR NOW.
ME TOO.

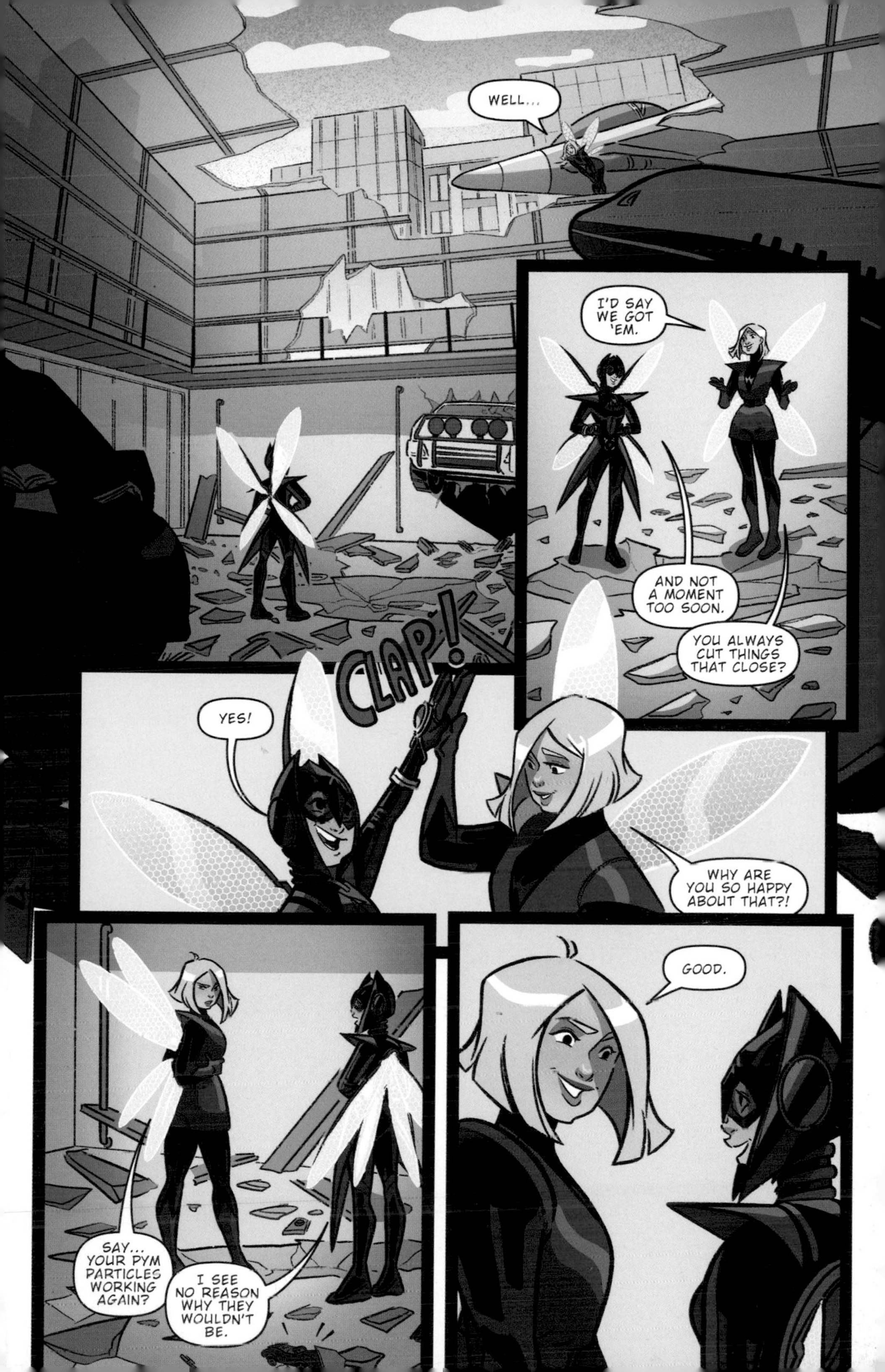
WELL...
I'D SAY WE GOT 'EM.
AND NOT A MOMENT TOO SOON.
YOU ALWAYS CUT THINGS THAT CLOSE?
CLAP!
YES!
WHY ARE YOU SO HAPPY ABOUT THAT?!
SAY... YOUR PYM PARTICLES WORKING AGAIN?
I SEE NO REASON WHY THEY WOULDN'T BE.
GOOD.

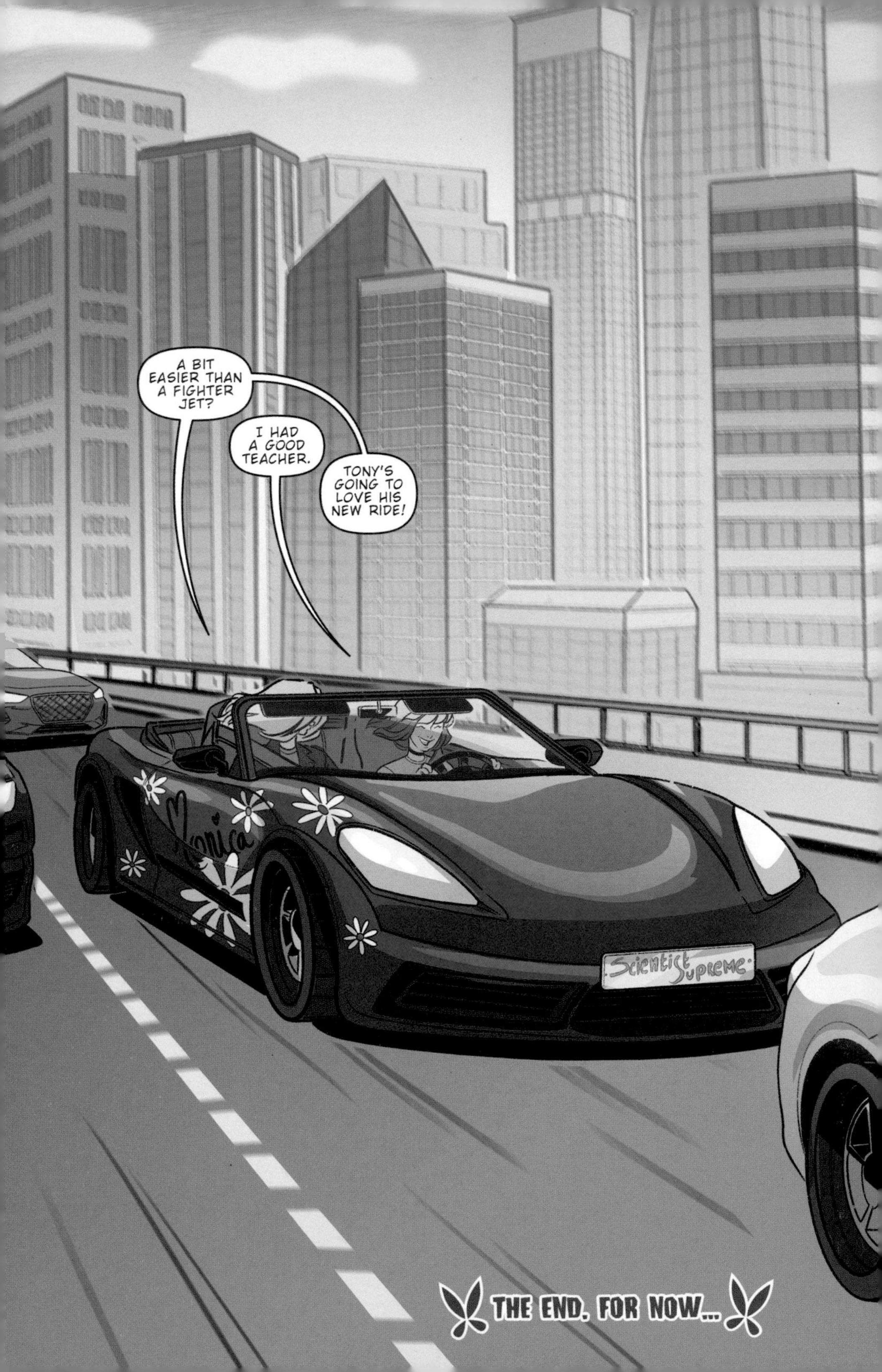
A BIT EASIER THAN A FIGHTER JET?
I HAD A GOOD TEACHER.
TONY'S GOING TO LOVE HIS NEW RIDE!
Monica
Scientist Supreme
THE END. FOR NOW...

ART BY: **SWEENEY BOO**

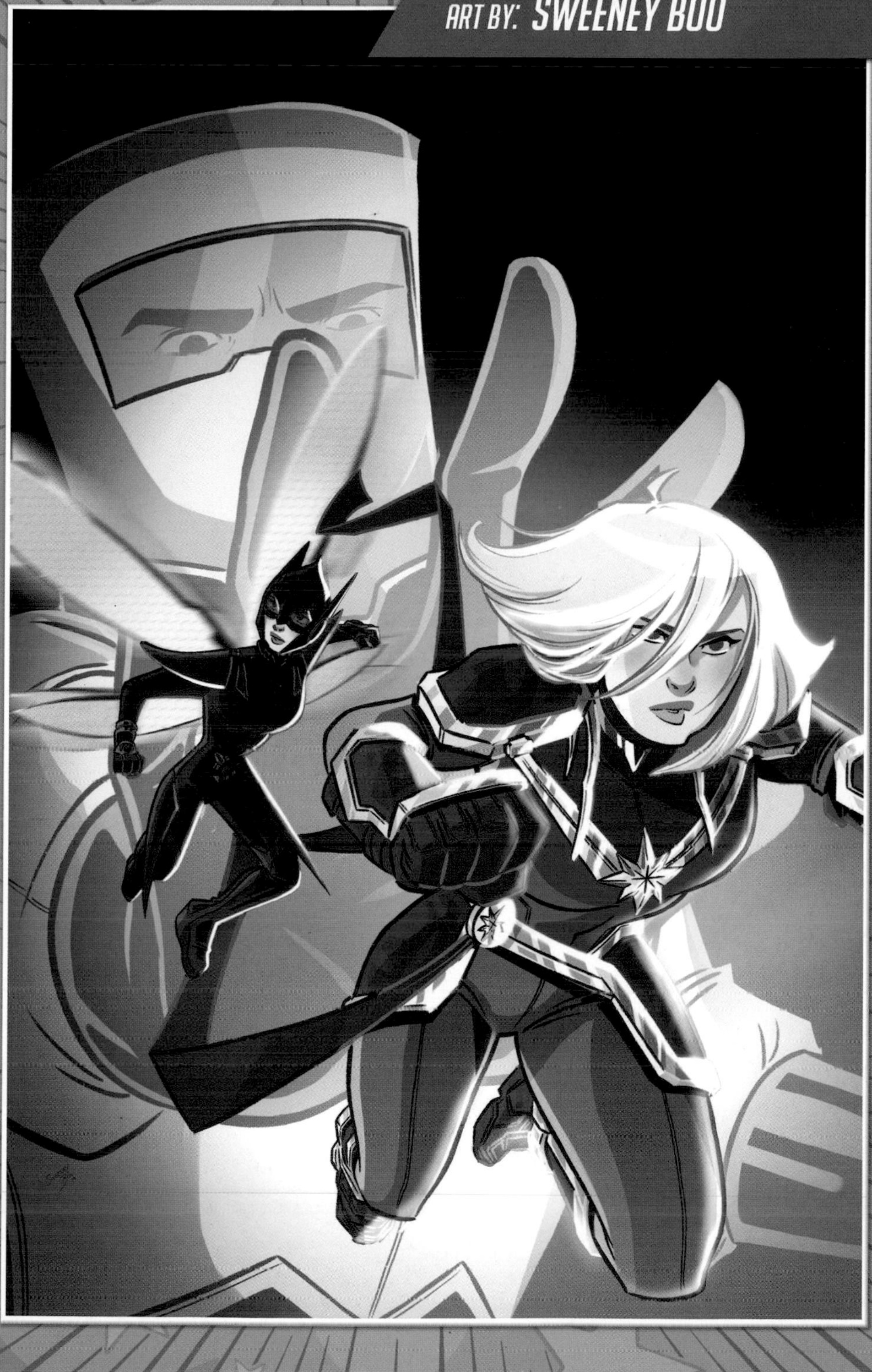

ART BY: KAREN HALLION

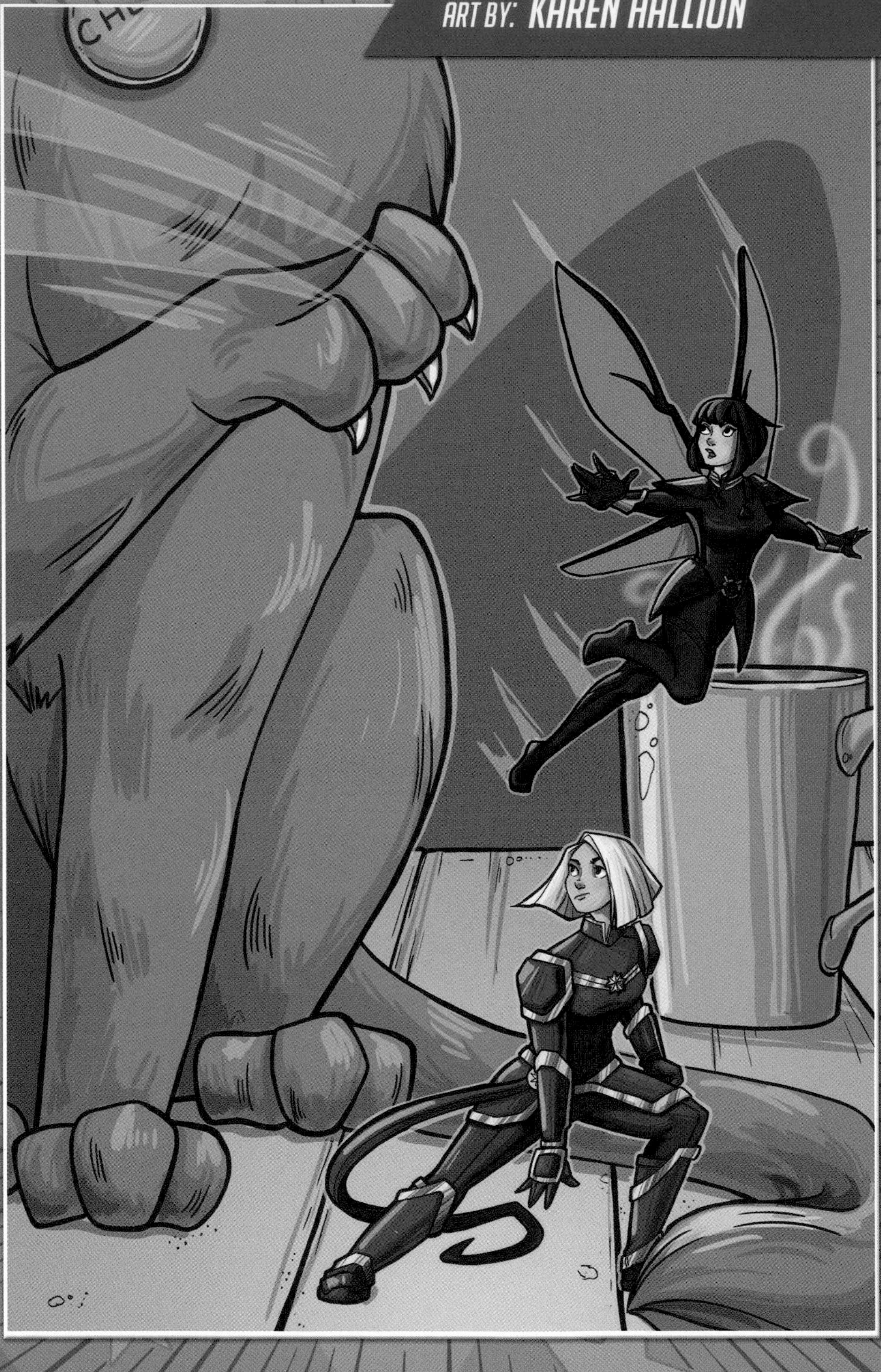

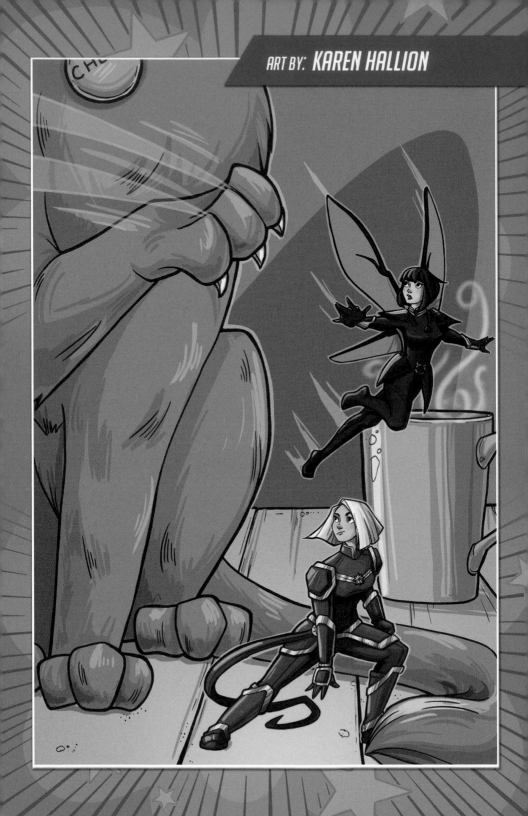